The Blue Diamond

Barrie McCappin

Blue Diamond

ISBN: 978-1-4716-9409-7

First publication in www.lulu.com

Copyright © Barrie McCappin 2012

Barrie McCappin has asserted his right under the Copyright, Designs and Patents Act 1988 to be identified as the author of this work.

In this work of fiction, the characters, places and events are either the product of the author's imagination or they are used entirely fictitiously. Any resemblance to actual persons living or dead, is purely coincidental.

This book is sold subject to the condition that it should, by way of trade or otherwise, be leant, resold, hired out, or otherwise circulated without the publisher's prior consent in any form of binding or cover other than that in which it is published and without a similar condition including this condition being imposed on the subsequent purchaser.

Barrie J McCappin was borne in 1940 at Aveley, Essex and now lives with his wife Daisy at Canvey Island. In the course of his working life he took occupations with firms of professional Quantity Surveyors and Building Contractors where he was employed on a number of large building and civil engineering projects. Now in retirement the Author spends his time in using his previous occupational skills in 'do it yourself' property enhancement and travelling. Author of the book 'Time for Change' he continues to write novels on fictitious situations in epochs within the twentieth and twenty first centuries.

Chapter 1 Released

Clank. The loud sound of the main prison doors closing on my release, sent a ray of hope in my mind that from then onwards everything was going to be fine. I wasn't sure what the future held for me, but I was determined that I would not repeat the experience of incarceration in this or any other of her majesty's establishments. Prison proved to be an environmental inconsistency of my life, which I was forced to endure as punishment. In fact I detested every minute of it and regularly counted the days until my release had become a reality. It did however cure me of one of my main habitual vices, which was the consumption of large quantities of alcohol, which prior to my punishment I would do on a regular daily basis much to the annoyance of my wife.

My name is Richard Wallace, although I prefer every one to call me Rick. I had served a period of six months for a crime of drink driving, which was not the first time I had been punished for the same offence. Other previous punishments meted out by the authorities were fines, endorsements on my licence or a complete restriction on my rights to drive a car. However this had been my first taste of penal reform and I was glad that it was well and truly behind me. I was now ready to face the future and the vagaries of a happier life. I am married with no children and no brothers or sisters. My mother and father moved to Australia five years ago. Apart from my wife and parents the only other relative I have is my grandmother Edith who is eighty five years of age.

There was a hoot of a car to gain my attention. It was my wife, Joy. I ran towards her clutching my meagre belongings and greeted her with a smile and a kiss. Her fresh faced complexion which was enhanced by green eyes and fair hair made her the envy of many of her friends. Through her twenty seven years she had managed to keep her slim figure and averaged height toned body, which she maintained through regular exercise. We had been married approximately six years before I was sentenced for my crime but I have to admit that the marriage wasn't exactly a happy one. We disagreed on many things and our squabbles would often lead to raging arguments. Throwing cups and saucers at one another was not an uncommon aspect of our married life together, so crockery was a regular item on our monthly purchase list.

Joy had always seemed cold and distant towards me and from the look on her face, together with her general body language, it didn't appear that she was pleased to see me again. It was noticeable when I was serving my time, that I didn't get many visits in prison from her and on the rare occasion that she made an appearance, there was never any admission that I was missed in any way. In fact we would often finish the prison visits with an argument about some minor triviality.

When we arrived home, the first thing I did was look in the hall mirror to see if prison had changed my physical appearance.   No,   I thought, I still looked my thirty three years of age with a pasty white complexion, still had all my jet black hair and my height still looked the same at six feet.   I smiled at the reflected image in the mirror pronouncing the deep dimple in my cheek, thinking in my vanity that if anything my appearance had improved.

I made my way to the lounge with the purpose of relaxing in a soft leather high back chair where I sat sipping a cup of tea and thankful I was resting back in my own comfortable home.   I glanced around the room to see if Joy had made any changes while I was away, when my eyes were immediately transfixed to the unusual pattern on the carpet.   This item was a new addition to our lounge.   I called out to Joy who was preparing dinner in the kitchen.

'Joy, you have changed the carpet in the lounge,' I called out.

'Yes,' she replied, 'do you like it?'

'I'm not so sure,' I said, 'it is very unusual and will take some getting used to. In fact I wished you had spoken to me first before you embarked on buying it.'

'Why would I want to speak to you about household furnishings, you were doing time for your uncontrollable drinking,' Joy pointed out.

Rather than create an argument about her purchase of this strange looking floor covering and my past drinking habit, I let the matter rest and continued to read my newspaper.

The carpet was a bright red with the pattern of a large blue jewel inlaid in the centre. The central image, was of a cut diamond portrayed from a side view elevation. Dimensions of the pattern were approximately two metres from head to the tapered base and approximately one metre wide. Like real diamonds this appeared to glisten as a result of a fluorescent light reflecting fabric and no matter where you turned your attention in the room, your eyes were subconsciously distracted and drawn towards it.

'I had the carpet specially made and being bespoke, there is not another one like it in the world,' she explained.

'Well I expect it will grow on me,' I sighed, 'but where did you get it?' I asked, curious to know who would sell such a peculiar type of floor covering.

'Oh, I bought it from Donald Jones, the carpet shop in the town,' replied Joy, 'all our friends like it, she continued.'

It was clear from the time I had arrived back home I wasn't getting much of a warm welcome. Joy remained distant and her indifference towards me was made apparent by her cold behaviour. However our cat Tibby was pleased to see me because he jumped on my lap and didn't seem to want to leave.

'It's time you went outside,' I said, at the same time picking up the cat off my lap and placing him outside the rear entrance door and into the garden.

As the evening wore on and nightfall approached, I was constantly distracted by the light reflected from the inlaid diamond on this carpet which acted like a luminous paint. With the ceiling light turned off, the whole pattern glistened enough to be a complete distraction, sufficient to interrupt my concentration whenever I found periods to sit and relax in the comfort of the lounge.

Chapter 2 The Intruder

In the excitement of being released from prison I decided to have an early night. I was so tired as a result of the events of the day, that sleep overcame me quickly and I did not hear Joy climb into bed beside me. It was so welcoming to doze off in a nice cosy bed instead of the uncomfortable bunks I was previously forced to endure provided by the prison establishment.

Around midnight, I was woken up by Joy nudging me forcefully in the back.

'What's the matter?' I asked turning over on my back and not at all happy that I had been disturbed in my sleep.

'Shush, be quiet, don't make so much noise, I think I can hear someone moving about downstairs,' she whispered, at the same time trembling with fear.

'No, that's only the wind,' I explained quietly and rolled over onto my side ready to succumb to be lost in further blissful slumber. At that moment there was a loud bang, as if something had been knocked on the floor. The noise resonated up the stairwell causing me to sit bolt upright in the bed.

'It could be Tibby. Did you put the cat out?' I asked Joy.

'No you did,' came the reply.

'Yes, I remember now, you're right, I did put him out,' I confirmed.

'There is someone else in the house, I think I can hear footsteps,' said Joy who by now was a complete bag of nerves.

Suddenly there was a bang and a clatter as if something had fallen or been knocked on the floor.

'That noise came from the kitchen,' whispered Joy.

'Yes, I think your right, it sounded like a saucepan had fallen over,' I whispered back, 'I'll investigate what is happening downstairs immediately.'

I put on some slippers and quietly, but gingerly walked down the stairs, gently stepping on each tread so as not to make a sound. When I was nearer to the bottom of the staircase, I could hear Joy following me, again stepping quietly on the treads. I made my way to the kitchen and with a sudden push on the handle, flung open the door but could not see anyone in the room. I was right, I noticed the saucepan on the floor which must have been the loud bang I had heard. Joy meanwhile had moved off in a different direction along the ground floor corridor towards the lounge.

'No!' I confirmed with a shout, 'there is nobody in here.'

I closed the kitchen door and was ready to retreat back to the warmth of my comfortable bed.

It was then when I heard this shrill piercing scream coming from within the lounge. It sounded like Joy and from the intensity of the scream it appeared she was in some kind of serious trouble.

I immediately retraced my steps to the kitchen and armed myself with a carving knife not knowing what to expect and ran towards the direction of the scream coming from the sitting room. When I entered the lounge, I noticed to my horror, a young man approximately seventeen years of age, with his hands clasped firmly around Joy's throat, obviously trying to either strangle her or stop the screaming she was making. I could see from Joy's face that she had gone a bluish colour and was losing consciousness. Grabbing hold of the man with both hands and holding the knife in my teeth, I tried to pull the intruder away from Joy but he would not loosen his grip, so without thinking about the consequences I didn't hesitate, I took the knife from my mouth and plunged it into the back of her attacker.

The intruder who was a large built man approximately six feet two inches released his grip, let out a cry, looked behind him and fell to the carpet in a heap like a stone. Blood was pouring profusely from his back and upper chest saturating the luminous blue diamond pattern on the carpet. I bent over the man to see if there was any movement in his rib cage to indicate any apparent inhalation or exhalation of air. I was satisfied that although in pain he was still breathing.

My attention was then drawn to Joy as I could hear her struggling to breath and coughing uncontrollably. I began by slapping her on the back, hoping that this would help her breathing.

'Are you alright?' I asked, noticing that Joy had a lot more blood on her pyjamas than I had on myself.

'Yes, I'm getting my breath back now. That was really terrifying,' she said. Joy looked across at me and then seeing the carving knife in my hand, asked, 'did you knife him?'

'Yes I did, it was the only way I could get him to release his grip, I was worried about you,' I replied, 'but we must do something about your attacker, he has obviously lost a lot of blood. Quick call a ambulance,' I shouted to Joy. My wife went over to the phone but in her panic dialled an incorrect number.

I turned the lad over, who opened his eyes and looked at me. At that moment I was relieved to see him still alive, although his breathing was a bit erratic and he was dribbling a lot. I did notice a knife lying on the floor, but this was some distance away from our attacker and wasn't sure if this was a weapon he had brought into the house.

'Don't let me die,' he said in a whimper as he clutched my pyjama jacket tightly with blooded hands.

I had forgotten about my anger in being terrorised by this young man and started to feel compassion towards him as he lay on the floor rolling from side to side, obviously in some pain. I tried to stem the blood escaping from his body by pressing hard against the wounds which was to his back and upper chest. However I could not understand how he had sustained a cut on the chest. The knife after all was not long enough to go right through his body and I hadn't exerted too much effort in my attack on his back.

'You will be okay,' I said reassuringly, 'try not to move, we will immediately get some medical help for you.'

'I'm in terrible pain,' said the attacker.

'Don't worry, help is on its way,' I assured him.

'Joy, have you dialled the emergency telephone number yet?' I asked in a panic.

Joy continued by attempting to redial the telephone number, but before she had completed, I noticed that our intruder had moved his head to one side and was no longer breathing or making any further effort to gain my attention. I frantically tried to shake him back to consciousness and when that didn't work tried mouth to mouth resuscitation, all of which proved ineffective in my efforts to remove him from his lifeless state.

'Stop,' I called out to Joy, 'It's too late. I think he has passed out, in fact I do believe he is dead.'

Joy did as instructed and replaced the telephone receiver.

'Dead? He can't be,' said Joy, who by this time had walked over to inspect the condition of the intruder. She bent down and went through all the procedures that I had gone through only to come to the same disastrous conclusion.

'What have you done?' she yelled hysterically.

My concern was so intense for this young man that I was unable to find a suitable answer to Joy's question. However I wasn't ready to accept my diagnostics or Joys and proceeded to work on this young man. I continued frantically to try to find a pulse on his wrist and listened for a heart beat, moving my right ear from one part of his body to another and back again. Alas, there was nothing to indicate a state of life. Pushing up and down on his rib cage to restart his heart and breathing proved ineffective. I then began to shake uncontrollably having come to the full realisation of the situation and the result of my impulsive actions.

My attention then transferred to my wife. Joy, by this time had stopped coughing and was again breathing normally. She had also calmed down from her hysterical behaviour. I left the intruder and went to check out Joy's injuries. Placing my hand on her chin, I turned her head from side to side looking all round her neck, which surprisingly had not a mark on it, neither did she have any physical damage on any other part of her body. I also noticed that I had not sustained any damage to my person either, not even a cut, a bruise or anything, although I, like Joy, did have a lot of the intruder's blood on my hands and clothes.

'Don't worry about me, concentrate on him,' bellowed Joy.

'It's no good, he is definitely dead,' I insisted.

'We must call the police and tell them what has happened,' screamed Joy as she paced up and down the lounge.

'Are you mad, have you thought this through?' I said, 'I have just come out of prison. I will get life for this.'

'How did he get in the house? There doesn't appear to be any breakages,' observed Joy.

I went into the kitchen and tried the back door to the garden which was unlocked.

'He must have come in through this door, I must have left the door unlocked when I put the cat out,' I said.

'Oh, you big idiot, so it's your fault that he managed to enter the house. Well what are we going to do? We can't leave him here on the floor,' shouted Joy.

' No, you're right. Listen, I can't make a decision in an instance. I must have some thinking time,' I replied, 'in the meantime we will put him in the garage until I decide what I am going to do.'

I rolled the patterned carpet around the intruder's body so that he was completely mummified in the roll and with the help of Joy dragged him along the floor through the rear door of the house, down the outside step and finally into the garage. By the time we had finished moving the corpse in the carpet the two of us were totally exhausted and gasping for breath. Suspecting that there was nothing else I could have done, I then followed Joy back to bed believing that things would look better in the morning.

With lack of sleep, tossing and turning in bed, I was worried about the events that had just occurred and at the same time trying to determine what I was going to do next. I noticed that Joy who once she had calmed down, seemed quite phlegmatic about the whole incident and had no problem sleeping.

The morning brought a stream of light coming through the window. I then realised that I must have fallen asleep through sheer tiredness, for a short period in the latter part of the morning.

'Was it a terrible dream I had had in the night? I was not certain.' Images started to flash through my mind. In the cold light of the day I had to check for myself that there was no reality to the nightmare that plagued my mind to absolute distraction. I crept out of bed and quietly descended the stairs, leaving Joy in a deep sleep.

I ran down the stairs and into the lounge and noticed by the visible appearance of bare floor boards that the diamond pattern carpet was missing. I continued into the garage fearful of what I was going to see next. The same carpet which had not received my unequivocal approval when I first noticed it, was rolled up and propped unceremoniously against the garage wall. I looked in the end of the roll and my worst fears were confirmed when I witnessed the gruesome sight I had tried so desperately to dismiss from my mind. A cold sweat had started to trickle down my back. *'No! It was not a bad dream, but what was I going to do?'* I thought to myself.

When I came in from the garage my entire body was shaking with the image in my mind of what I had just seen. Joy by this time had removed herself from her bed, dressed herself and was in the kitchen making some tea.

'You have been away from here such a long time I can't remember if you take sugar with your tea?' requested Joy.

'What?' I said as I looked up at her in a daze, as if in another world, not hearing anything that had been said to me. Joy looked at me and realised that I was lost in my own confused thoughts and repeated the question.

'No! In all the time I have known you, I have never taken sugar with my tea,' I answered.

Joy picked up on my unusual uncharacteristic mannerisms and tried to give me advice.

'You really must inform the police and tell them what has happened here,' Joy said.

'No!' I replied stubbornly, 'I really could not face the rigours of prison again and I would certainly be facing a long stretch with this one.'

'But you were acting in self defence, I'm sure in mitigation, the authorities will understand that,' replied Joy.

'That's wishful thinking. Listen Joy, there was a well publicised case in the newspaper last year in 1999, when a young teenager was shot from behind for entering a farmer's property in Norfolk. He was killed with a bullet in his back by the owner of the property. Against public opinion and the actions of pressure groups, the farmer was eventually convicted to life imprisonment. I can not see any difference between that case and what happened last night, with the only exception being, a knife was used on the back of the victim instead of the bullet from a firearm. As for explaining that it was self defence, this could be difficult because neither of us has suffered any apparent physical injuries.'

'What is going to happen about our diamond patterned carpet? It's ruined,' said Joy.

With the circumstances we were faced with I was surprised that Joy was so concerned about her precious floor covering.

'Well, you can forget about the carpet, that is the last thing on my mind. In any case it is so heavily blood stained that it can no longer serve any useful purpose,' I replied.

'We can't leave a dead body in the garage,' Joy shouted.

'No we can't, you are absolutely right, we will move it tonight under the cover of darkness,' I replied.

'We? There is not going to be any 'we' about it. You did this on your own Rick, so you can get out of this on your own, I don't want anything to do with it,' Joy urged emphatically.

'I can not do this on my own,' I replied, 'I really do need some physical help. Remember, if it had not been for me, our intruder may have strangled you.'

'Oh dear. What have you got me into here,' sighed Joy, 'this seems like a bit of emotional blackmail.'

'Joy, what happened to the other knife?' I asked, 'it seems to have disappeared.

'What knife?' she queried.

'There was a knife lying in the corner of the lounge on the floor. Did it belong to the intruder?' I asked.

'No,' she said, 'I remember, it was one of our cutlery knives. I washed it up and put it back in the draw,' confirmed Joy.

I couldn't be certain, because I was sure it wasn't a cutlery knife, but had no reason to doubt what Joy was saying and didn't pursue her with any further questions.

During the evening at approximately eleven o'clock, I persuaded Joy to help me move the body into the boot of the car. Both the body and the car were in the garage, so I knew that no other person could witness what we were doing. Our main problem in moving the contents for our car boot was that the carpet was almost as heavy as the man inside it. Also the bulk was so large that we had to let down the back seat to accommodate our load. We both struggled with the heavy weight, which we first managed to support on the edge of the opened car boot and then gradually inch by inch move the whole load into the car.

As far as Joy was concerned, she had fulfilled all that she was going to do as an accomplice, telling me in no uncertain terms that I was now very much on my own as she wanted no further involvement.

I drove off in the car not knowing where I was heading. The only thing I did know was that I had to get rid of my cargo and dispose of it quickly and without attention of others. I continued driving and noticed that I was in unfamiliar territory, but road signs indicated I was on the A3 heading towards Guildford.

My headlights picked out someone standing in the road, who was attempting to flag me down. As I approached nearer I noticed it was a man who was trying to stop my vehicle. Normally I wouldn't stop in instances like this and would usually take avoiding action by driving round him. However in this case I was forced to stop. To do otherwise would have caused an accident.

Breaking hard I noticed that there were some people at the side of the road and someone lying on the edge of the road who was obviously in some kind of distress.

When my vehicle came to a halt, the man came round the side of the car and put his head in the window.

'I wonder if you can help us?' he enquired.

'Why, what's the matter? I asked.

'There is a lady at the side of the road who has had a terrible accident. Have you got a mobile phone?' he enquired.

'Yes I have,' I replied.

'Can you phone the emergency services, because I need to get this lady to hospital quickly,' he said.

I did what I was asked to do and walked over to the young woman who was screaming in agony. I noticed a lot of blood coming from her leg. Removing a handkerchief from my pocket, I rolled it up to act as a tourniquet and wrapped it tightly around the upper part of her leg. She was clearly in a lot of pain and I tried to make her as comfortable as possible.

We didn't have to wait long before an ambulance arrived and she was quickly removed. Considering I had achieved all that I could have done, I went straight over to the car and got inside it, when a police vehicle prevented me from driving away.

'Wait a minute, please sir,' said the officer, 'can you please get out of your car and follow me.'

I did as he requested. He then walked over to the two crashed vehicles in the accident. One was caved in at the front and the other badly dented in the back.

'Can I have your name please,' said the officer.

In consideration of my nasty secret, I was reluctant to give my name.

'Why do you want my details? I wasn't a witness to this accident,' I answered.

'Then what are you doing here?' asked the officer.

'I was merely flagged down to help. I was the one who was instrumental in phoning you,' I replied.

'That's right,' said the man who flagged me down.

'You can go then,' said the officer.

Heaving a sigh of relief, I walked away from the scene of the accident. Thankful to get back in my car, I continued my interrupted drive.

I hadn't driven far when it was necessary to slow my vehicle down because the car was coasting me over to the left. Pulling in off the road I went to investigate my mechanical problem, which happened to be a puncture on the front nearside wheel.

This was one time that I didn't want to do running repairs. I proceeded to remove my toolkit from the boot and started to remove the road wheel when I heard the screech of tyres through heavy breaking and a man getting out of his car.

'What's the matter mate. Can I help,' asked the young man, who by this time had started to lift the lid of the car boot.

'What are you doing?' I asked, worried that he might discover the contents in the back of my car.

'I'm getting the spare wheel out for you,' he said.

'No, you can't, there is a carpet in there,' I replied.

'Oh, I'll soon move that,' he said.

He proceeded to move the carpet.

'Gosh, this is heavy. Have you got a body in here or something?' he asked.

'Oh, very funny,' I replied.

He continued to proceed to pull at the carpet.

'No,' I insisted, 'leave it alone, and I'll thank you to mind your own business.'

My abrupt rudeness directed at my helper, caused him to push back the carpet, that he had disturbed, to its original position and slam the car boot closed in apparent annoyance.

'You are touchy, some people are glad of roadside assistance. I don't think I want to help you now anyway,' he replied.

My interfering helper then got into his car and drove off at speed, giving me a vulgar two finger salute as he left. I wasn't phased by his insulting behaviour, but relieved that I had managed to rid myself of him and apply full concentration on what I had to do.

One thing I did discover having removed the front wheel, was that I couldn't get to the spare wheel because of the body lying over it. Weighing up the situation I came to the full realisation that I had to remove the body from the boot take out the spare wheel and put the body back in the car again. I didn't think that I had the physical strength to carry out all these tasks, plus this would have most certainly attracted the attention of passing motorists and the last thing I wanted was the infiltration of human interest. I was beginning to think that there were forces I didn't understand conspiring against me with all these interruptions occurring in close succession. Was it a form of punishment for my dreadful crime?

I looked around and saw that I had stopped outside a farmer's field which was partially hidden by a row of trees. This was the first bit of good fortune that had come my way and seemed to solve two of my problems, because I could bury the body just the other side of the trees and once I had removed my rather unpleasant cargo, I could then take out the spare wheel and complete the replacement.

Directing my eyes all around me, I found that there was no one I could see in the immediate vicinity and grabbed myself a spade from my vehicle and preceded to dig a hole big enough to accommodate the unpleasant contents in my car boot. The ground being wet heavy clay, made digging slow and difficult and although I worked as hard and as fast as I could, the excavation seemed to take an eternity. During the effort expended in covering up my felony, I could feel the perspiration dripping off me. I knew this to be as a result more of worry, than as a cause of the expenditure of effort I was putting into the digging.

Having dug the grave, I had to move the body which was wrapped in the carpet. I opened the car boot and feverishly pulled at the carpet, which I managed to drag onto the ground with one exerted tug. A loud thud was caused as the weight of the carpet and its contents hit the ground. The force of the fall onto the hard clay ground, opened the carpet slightly displaying the illuminated blue diamond and the horror it was hiding. I looked around to see if anyone had been attracted by this sudden influx of reflected light from the carpet and quickly rolled it up to mask my secret. I could see headlights from vehicles passing on the main road and hoped I couldn't be seen. However, I was partly shielded by a row of trees adjacent to the road. Away from the road were open fields, so this exposed area became my main concern in being noticed. Fortunately I couldn't see anyone, so I continued by dragging the carpet, finally dropping it and its contents into the newly dug grave.

As I started to backfill the hole with soil to an uncompleted depth of six inches, I was mortified to note the blue diamond pattern of the carpet was showing through the soil. I frantically added more clay and was relieved when I could no longer see it and prayed that no one would stop to witness what I was doing. I continued backfilling to a depth of four feet careful in replacing topsoil and vegetation last so as to prevent any detection of soil disturbance.

Returning to my car, I started the car and engaged a gear and suddenly remembered that I had not put the replacement road wheel on the car and almost drove the car off of the supporting jack. Replacing a wheel in the dark was difficult and prevented my quick retreat. I counted myself fortunate that in the time I was working on the car no one stopped to give me a hand or talk to me.

I drove away and headed back home and took some solace that I had covered my tracks well, which I hoped was the last I would experience of this nightmare incident. What gave me serious cause for concern was that apart from being involved in a criminal act, I was now thinking like a criminal by making careful and calculated decisions on the method of hiding my felony. This was totally contrary to my character as a person, as I had never remotely been involved in anything violent before in my life. However I could not get out of my mind the events of the last twenty four hours and hoped that in due time I would forget that this surreal part of my life had ever happened.

Chapter 3 Employment

My trade before incarceration was a skilled bricklayer, which I was happy to pursue and embrace again if the right conditions and opportunities presented themselves, but wondered if my speed of laying bricks and quality of work had been affected after the nine months taken up by my term of imprisonment. I trawled the local building sites in the newspaper and with a bit of travelling found a suitable job where a bricklaying foreman was happy to engage me purely on experience and fortunately not on proof of background. I was fearful about anyone knowing about my chequered past, and preferred to keep this as a closely guarded secret.

I thought that in getting gainful employment, my mind would be occupied on my work instead of the dreadful situation in which I had placed myself and the demons which were constantly playing with my mind and putting me under extreme stress.

The foreman's name was Peter Brown. At six foot two inches, Peter, who was approximately forty five years of age, stood two inches above me. He had a friendly face with a ruddy outdoor wind swept complexion, a balding head and dark brown eyes. From the moment he employed me as part of one of the construction gangs we became firm friends. He would often lumber his overweight frame towards me and chat about anything, even topics which were not work related. Eventually when it was found that we had common interests in golf, old cars and social drinking, we would meet up at regular intervals outside of our working hours. As the building progressed, I was aware that Peter would always treat me with some favouritism by giving me the jobs where maximum money could be earned. Despite his weight, he enjoyed a game of golf and often asked me to accompany him. It became evident to the rest of the workforce that we were inseparable.

Then one day I invited Peter and his wife Dianne over for dinner. When they arrived I was surprised and delighted to learn that Joy and Dianne knew one another. It made the conversation easier without the need for all round introductions.

'I see that you have changed your carpet,' said Dianne looking down at the plain red carpet.

'Yes, you're right,' replied Joy surprised at the question, 'you're very observant, fancy you noticing that.'

'The other carpet had a distinctive blue diamond, that's why I remember it,' remarked Dianne. 'What made you get rid of it?'

'Oh, it had a nasty stain on the pattern which I could not remove, so we had to throw the carpet away,' explained Joy.

'I think I prefer the other one you had, I was talking to Peter about it suggesting that we get one like it,' said Dianne.

Although in many respects Joy's comments were true, I wanted to get off the taboo subject of carpets for obvious reasons. The mere mention of the word brought a shudder down my spine, so I quickly changed the topic to something less distressing.

'Do you have any children? I asked Dianne.

'Yes, we have a boy and a girl,' replied Dianne. The girl is aged fourteen years and we have no problems with her. The boy is aged seventeen and has a totally different character and you could say a complete drop out from society. He moves from one piece of trouble to another and we live in fear of what he is going to do next. He gets caught up in fights, has been involved in theft, does drugs and is well known to the police. I can't understand him. He never used to be like this. I think that in the past he has mixed with the wrong crowd. In fact I will give you an example. Twenty four hours ago he had a big row with Peter and we haven't seen him since. It is just typical of what he does. He just packed a few things and left the house, not even telling us if we would see him again. He has done this before. We are not too concerned as we know he will soon come back when he is hungry, but he won't apologise. That I do know.'

'Has he got a job,' I asked.

'No, he has never worked before in his life, a real dropout in society. He expects Peter and me to keep him, but I can assure you that will not happen for much longer,' reported Dianne.

'I don't think I have ever seen him, but there again I wouldn't know him if I saw him,' I said.

'Oh, you must have noticed him before, he is a big lad and has been living in this town a long time, his name is Ralph,' said Dianne.

'No, the name does not ring any bells with me,' I replied.

'Wait,' Dianne continued, 'I have a recent photograph of my two children in my handbag.'

Dianne moved over to her handbag which was lying on a vacant chair, removed a snapshot of her two children and passed it to both Joy and myself to look at. I noticed that the girl was very similar in appearance to Dianne, displaying a large frame, a long nose and a similar height of approximately five foot one inch. My eyes then turned to the lad in the photograph. I was startled to observe that I recognised him as the intruder who had recently broken into our house. My immediate change of manner of surprise brought a quick reaction from Peter.

'Are you alright old boy?' he asked, 'you have gone all white in fact you look as though you have seen a ghost.'

'It's nothing,' I said trying to regain my composure, 'I suddenly came over all faint, but I think I'm alright now.'

'Sit down, take it easy you've probably been over doing it, I know I've been pushing you hard at work, but I didn't realise that it would have this effect on you,' said a rather concerned Peter.

I desperately tried to compose myself and divert the attention away from me.

'Well, have you seen either of my two children around in the town,' Dianne asked.

'I don't recognise the young lady in the photograph but I do believe I have seen the lad somewhere before,' I admitted.

Throughout the rest of the evening I could think of nothing else other than the person I recognised in the photograph. I was entertaining the parents of someone that I had killed in my house, exchanging pleasantries with them and they had no idea. Worst still, I had to go to the building site the next day and continue working with Peter, who still had no knowledge that his son would never return. I tried to imagine what they would do if they knew the awful truth.

I was glad when our guests decided to leave, as their presence was making me feel uncomfortable and a constant reminder of that terrible night in June.

'Joy, did you notice the lad in that photograph, Dianne showed us?' I asked.

'No, I wasn't paying too much attention. Do you know him?' she enquired.

'Unfortunately I do and so do you. It was the same person who broke into our house the other night,' I confirmed.

'What are you sure?' yelled Joy, 'It can't be,' said Joy doubting the reality of the situation.

'Oh, I'm sorry to say that there is no possibility that I am wrong, having spent so much time in trying to revive him, I would recognise him anywhere,' I argued.

'If you are right, that's a terrible situation made worse. We will lose Peter and Dianne as friends. What are we going to do now?'

'We will have to move from the area. I can not stay in this house for much longer, it is a constant reminder of what I have done,' I sighed.

'Do you mean we must sell up because you have done something stupid?' asked Joy.

'That's exactly what I do mean,' I replied, 'I will put the house up for sale the day after tomorrow. Also another thing I can't continue to work with Peter for obvious reasons, so I will have to terminate my employment with him as soon as possible. I will tell him at the end of the week.'

The next day, I was back at work. Peter greeted me with a smile and gave me some facing brickwork to execute, although my mind was everywhere but on what I was doing. Such was distress that my work was suffering prompting Peter to come over and give me a good ticking off.

'These bricks you have laid today are not up to your usual standard of workmanship,' he said as he pointed to an area of the wall.

I looked at my work and couldn't believe my eyes. The 'perps' or vertical joints for my last two courses were not staggered as is normal practise, but in a straight line. Peter was right I had never ever built a wall so badly since I joined the trade. I felt ashamed at what I had done and immediately removed the freshly laid brickwork, apologising as I tried to remedy my poor workmanship.

'That's alright,' said Peter, 'try not to do that again, I don't want the Clerk of the Works complaining about us to the Main Contractor.'

At lunch, Peter, the person I was trying to avoid all day due to my embarrassment, came and sat by my side, which was the last thing I wanted.

'You remember what we were talking about yesterday,' said Peter.

'No, remind me,' I replied hoping that he was not about to mention his missing son.

'My son Ralph has not returned,' advised Peter, 'I know what he is trying to do, he is trying to teach me a lesson for arguing with him the other night. Well it's not going to work, he must learn to respect his elders,' he added stubbornly.

'Also, when he does return, I'm going to make him find a job. I've offered to teach him bricklaying, but he is not interested, he doesn't want to do anything,' continued Peter.

At this juncture I did not know what to say to him, so I remained silent, gazing at the ground and only gave slight nods in acknowledgement to his questions. Then the discomfort of the conversation overcame me and I had to make an excuse to move away.

'I'm sorry Peter, I had better get back to that wall I so badly ruined and catch up on some wasted time,' I said, as my voice tailed off to something barely audible.

I was glad to see the working day finished so that I could get away from Peter, who seemed obsessed with the argument he had with his son and what he was going to make him do when he returned home.

The following day I put the house on the market and gave notice of my intention to leave my employment to Peter. Peter couldn't understand why I had come to my conclusions and was sorry I was no longer part of his workforce.

The day after seeing Peter, the local newspaper was pushed through the letter box which Joy managed to retrieve before I could get to it.

'Have a look,' at this said Joy, 'I told you that you aught to contact the local police station, instead of acting like some form of no good vigilante.' At that moment in fit of anger, she thrust the newspaper against my body.

On the front page was the picture to which I had now become very familiar, displaying Ralph Brown with his sister, or Peter and Dianne's son and daughter. It described Ralph as a missing teenage person who had not been seen for over a week. It also added that if anyone knew of his whereabouts, they should contact either Peter Brown or the local Police station.

I pondered over what Joy had said, but knew that I could not confess to what I had done, which was compounded when I hid the evidence.

'Joy, I'm aware that you are probably right, but I can't face prison again. In any case you have been compliant in everything I have done and assisted me on occasion,' I confided.

'I'm well aware of that,' replied Joy, 'and that is why I will not tell anyone about what has happened, but I further inform you that as far as I am concerned, you are on your on own in this.'

Joy having made her position perfectly clear in taking this stance, only increased my disappointment and I realised that I really was alone to cope with the problem.

Chapter 4 Press Coverage

One week had elapsed since giving up my job, when I received a knock on the door. It was Peter.

My eyes rolled in disbelief when I saw him and I wasn't in any position to have any cosy chats. I had an idea why he had called, as I thought he would try again to persuade me to return to his bricklaying workforce.

'Hello Rick,' he said in his usual friendly manner, 'I thought I'd come round and see how you are, also see if I can persuade you to return to your old job, we are desperate to find tradesmen of your calibre.'

'The problem is, I shall soon be moving out of the locality and that was the reason I resigned. It would be better if I was to wait until I changed areas and then find local work,' I replied.

Although I had always been friends with Peter, my circumstances were such that I did not want him to call on me or see him socially any more. I felt uncomfortable in his presence and was unable to converse with him in the way that I had become accustomed. I certainly didn't want to discuss the problems he was having with his son.

'Aren't you going to invite me in?' asked Peter who appeared surprised that after a long uncomfortable silence he had to be proactive to raise the question.

'Well I am in a bit of a hurry, but please do come in,' I replied, anxiously hoping that his visit would not be too long. We walked into the lounge and I offered him a chair, whereupon the dreaded subject of Ralph was again resurrected.

'Remember I told you that my son had walked out. Well, it is now two weeks since I last saw him and as a result of this long lapse in time I getting very concerned. He has never left home for as long as this before. I have even contacted some of his friends and they have not seen him either, which is most unusual,' advised Peter.

'Oh dear,' I replied, 'I don't know what to suggest.'

'Well, I have initiated a bit of local press coverage and if this does not work I will have to go global. Media attention often brings about results,' said Peter.

I felt a certain unease run through my body regarding the actions already in place by Peter. Also the moves he intended to process if local media did not produce any quick or satisfying results.

'Have you recently cut yourself,' enquired Peter.

'Not that I'm aware,' I confirmed. 'Why do you ask?'

'Because you have splatters of blood on your wallpaper over there,' remarked Peter.

My eyes followed in the same direction of Peter's sight level. I was mortified to see that there were spots of dried blood that had come from Ralph I hadn't noticed before, which was not just on the wallpaper that Peter had noticed, but also very visible on the white skirting board. I tried to hide my reaction of obvious surprise.

'Oh, that,' I assured, 'that has been there for some time. I had not got around to removing it.'

My answer seemed to satisfy Peter's curiosity because there was no further follow up on his discovery and he completely changed the subject.

'Well, I only came around to see if I could persuade you to take your old job back, but as you have made up your mind and there appears no way that I can change it, I will quietly leave,' said Peter.

I showed Peter to the door said my goodbyes and hoped that he was not going to become a regular visitor to my house.

*

The lack of employment caused our finances to plummet drastically, which had the effect of household bills piling up. Joy in the meantime was getting extremely depressed and didn't actually enjoy the constant companionship of me being home all of the time. However, we did have some good news in finding a buyer for our property, so I knew it wouldn't be long before we were on the move.

I was pleased to relate to Joy the news, at the same time informing her that we had to start looking for another house. I was surprised to learn that Joy was unconcerned by my news and began by telling me of her own life changing plans.

'I have decided that I am going to leave you and make a new life of my own,' said Joy.

This was a complete shock and caught me completely unawares.

'What has brought this on? This is a surprise completely out of the blue. Why, is there someone else?' I asked.

'No there is no one else. I just can't stand you moping about in a world of your own, creating an uncomfortable atmosphere and generally making everyone miserable around you. Life has certainly not been pleasant here lately,' explained Joy.

I realised what she was saying was right, I had become a bit of a recluse in my own little world, although this had been brought on by worry, the guilt of what I had done and concern for the future.

'Where will you go?' I asked in a concerned manner.

'I am going to stay with my sister Sylvia,' replied Joy.

'But you don't get on with her and you are always moaning about her,' I pointed out.

'Oh, don't you worry about that,' she said, 'I have asked her if I could stay there and that's exactly what I am going to do,' insisted Joy.

I was saddened by this decision, and watched unable to speak, as she packed suitcases in front of me and calmly walked out of the house closing the door gently behind her. Although the romance had gone out of the marriage and our relationship had become a bit stale, I nevertheless did not think she would leave me. Neither did I want us to separate. However, I knew that Joy living with her twin sister Sylvia would never work as they constantly argued and neither one would succumb to an admission of wrongdoing.

The house was now in an eerie silence, leaving me alone with my thoughts. Yes, I had plenty of thoughts to contemplate, all of them sinking me further and further into deep depression.

As the days went by I had received no telephone calls or any other form of communication from Joy, I then knew that she had definitely made up her mind and was not coming back.

Five weeks after Joy had left me, I was packing all my belongings into boxes ready to move out. I was in many ways relieved, because any time I sat in the lounge, I was reminded of that fateful night which I relived in my thoughts over and over again.

I sent half of the money I received from the sale of the property to Joy, who surprisingly was still staying with her sister Sylvia. I retained my contribution for paying old debts and finding a place to rent.

The one thing I wanted to do was move away from my current locality and start a new life. After much searching I found myself a one bedroom bungalow to rent, which was approximately seventy miles from my old address. I felt that this was far enough away from Peter and Dianne Brown and also satisfied my current modest requirements.

It was now time to put my bricklaying skills to good use and find myself some employment with a trade subcontractor. My searching was not in vain because I was soon back on a building site doing what I knew best.

The move into a new address in a different locality was quite therapeutic, because I found that my guilty secret was not constantly on my mind and I was able to apply a higher level of concentration to my routine daily activities. The dreadful memories of that awful June night, was gradually being eclipsed by time.

The first job I was given in my new occupation was to construct the brick shell extension to a solicitor's office. I tried to make this job last a long time, because there was a young female solicitor by the name of Alice to whom I had become friendly. It was the one thing that I needed was the company of another person to stabilise my life and return me to being a normal human person again. At age twenty seven, she was seven years younger than me, had dark brown hair which was straight and long, flowing over her shoulders. She had a slim body of average height and large pale blue eyes.

It was of great disappointment to me when the contract started to come to a close because I knew I would not see her again. I decided to invite her out to dinner just before my work on the site had finished and was surprised, but delighted when she accepted my proposal. I was determined to make the most of our date which was scheduled for the following day.

When the day of our dinner date arrived I took Alice to an Indian Restaurant in the middle of town. At dinner, Alice explained to me that her work often took her to court in order to represent clients. I could see that in meeting up with this young lady I was going to be educated in legal processes old and current that had occurred throughout the country and duly prepared myself for long chats on the subject of British law.

As time progressed, Alice's conversation had become a trifle boring which continued with the same similar theme on legal processes, to the extent that I tended to only half listen to what she had to say. Then just when I thought the ennui of her domineering sole subject chatting was getting the better of me, she said something that immediately drew my full attention.

'Did you see this morning's paper about a murder that had taken place in the Guildford area?' asked Alice.

Alice by now had attained complete control of the conversation as she related to me in intricate detail the substance of what she had read in the newspaper. Cold sweat ran down the back of my neck on hearing the words 'murder' and 'Guildford' in the same sentence.

'No, I must confess I had not seen the newspaper today,' I replied. I noticed a tremor in my voice which Alice picked up on.

'Are you alright,' she said in a rather concerned manner, 'I thought you were going to faint, which would have been dreadful because it would have meant that I would be left with our dinner bill,' she added jokingly.

'No I'm okay,' I said composing myself, at the same time giving a nervous faked chuckle at what she thought was an amusing remark.

'What did the newspaper say about the murder?' I said eager to learn more.

'Oh, only that a man had confessed to killing his wife, but could not remember where he had disposed of the body,' related Alice.

'What do mean he could not remember?' I asked relieved that it was something unrelated to my own guilty secret.

'Well, that is the curious part of it,' said Alice, 'he knew that he had buried her in a farmer's field but did not know which field.'

'That's an incredible story. What is going to happen now?' I asked.

'The newspaper didn't report that. However I am confident there will be a search,' said Alice. Can you imagine it. There are lots of fields around Guildford. It will be like finding a needle in a haystack.

'Farmers' fields?' I queried.

'Yes, surrounding Guildford,' Alice reiterated.

With all your legal knowledge, do you think they will find her?' I asked inquisitively.

'Oh, they will find her alright,' replied Alice, 'they have helicopters with special surveillance equipment which can detect soil disturbance from the air.'

'When do you think they will start this process?' I asked.

'I'm not sure, but I am certain they won't waste any time. They may possibly start tomorrow,' replied Alice.

'Anyway I'm only guessing, I don't really know. Why do you ask?' said Alice.

'I just like to know how police deal with searches of that nature,' I replied.

Although I was listening intently to everything Alice was saying I was not enjoying this conversation at all. In fact I could see I was not going to relish the rest of my dinner date, or appreciate the company of my beautiful guest. The food I was eating was already beginning to taste insipid due to a sudden influx of disturbed thoughts. I thought hard about the possible scenarios which could be uncovered by the police. If they found the body of the murdered lady first, then they would have no reason to look further. However, if they found Ralph first, then that would promote another enquiry for them.

I also thought that whatever they found in what order, they had no reason to link anything to me. Then I began to remember about the unique purpose made carpet displaying the florescent blue diamond that Joy had ordered. The neighbours knew I had it, along with Peter and Dianne Brown, also the local carpet dealer must have remembered such a distinct order. If the police stumbled across this unusual floor covering, they could easily link it back to me or Joy, the purchaser. Under such circumstances I would be indeed a marked man.

'Look Alice,' I said, 'do you mind if we end the evening early, that is as soon as we finish our meal. The reason is that I am not feeling very well. I think it could possibly be a cold or flu coming on.'

'I thought you looked a bit off colour,' Alice replied, 'Of course you must take me back home right away if you are not feeling too well.'

I was glad that Alice took my excuses so understandably, and was relieved when I was able to say my goodbyes to her. It was also relieving to escape her constant banter on the law. However had she not mentioned the unrelated case of the missing wife in Guildford I would probably have completed eating my Indian meal instead of leaving half of it on the plate.

The drive home was full of thoughts on what I was going to do next. Whatever was going through my mind I knew I couldn't leave the body of Ralph in the Guildford area. He had to be moved and quickly. In fact I had no time to lose, believing that I had to do it that day under the cover of darkness.

Chapter 5 Moving the Evidence

I arrived home really tired through worry, but my first thoughts were to get to Ralph's resting place as soon as I possibly could. I decided it would be more convenient for reason of space and easier rear vehicle door access, to take the builder's van the subcontractor had loaned me and head off to Guildford as soon as I could.

When I arrived at the field, I had great difficulty in finding the exact location of my previous excavation. The realisation that I had covered my tracks well, served no useful purpose at all in rediscovering the spot where I had previously made my excavation. Wandering around the approximate location brought back dreadful memories of the time I first buried him and a shudder down my spine.

I thought I knew of the approximate location and tried my luck. I found what I believed to be some backfilled earth and began to frantically dig at the soil. The excavation was a lot easier than before because the earth had not been completely compacted.

I dug down to a depth of four feet and noticed the edge of a carpet. This indicated to me that I was in approximately the correct spot, but had to move my excavation sideways a few feet. All the time I was digging I was looking around me and praying that any of the cars that were racing down the A3 arterial road would not see my parked vehicle or the dimly lit torch that I placed shining down from a tree branch. The last thing I wanted was for a vehicle to stop and investigate what I was doing.

Finally I was alerted by the florescent shine of the diamond pattern on the carpet and dug around so that the full roll of this floor covering was exposed. Being hit by the very unpleasant smell of the body which by this time had partly decomposed was not what I was expecting, although it did confirm that I was in the exact location. The stench was so bad that I was overcome with a nauseous reaction. It made my stomach reach to the extent that I was eventually physically sick behind one of the trees.

I told myself that however unpleasant, I had to do this. Without stopping to think about my actions, I dragged the carpet and its contents out of the excavation and then with further exertion, lifted the combined load into the back of the van. I then started to backfill the excavation I had dug.

Halfway through the backfill I was startled by car headlights of a vehicle which was decelerating and then finally stopping yards from where I was digging. A middle aged man got out of his car and walked behind the trees where I was shovelling soil.

'What are you doing?' he said, looking suspiciously at the hole.

'Oh I've just buried a pet dog here,' I replied.

'It must have been a mighty big dog, that's a big hole you've dug here,' he said.

'Yes, it was, it was a Great Dane, I had a job lifting it into the hole,' I replied.

'Do you want a hand?' he asked, 'I've got a spade in the van and I can help you backfill.'

'No thank you,' I replied hoping my answer would deter him and he would soon be on his way.

'You won't tell anyone about this will you, because I don't think that I am supposed to do this,' I urged.

'Nothing to do with me mate,' he replied.

'Anyway, why have you stopped?' I asked.

'Oh, I just want to relieve myself,' he answered. He immediately went over to one of the trees to ease his discomfort.

'Oh, No!', he yelled, 'someone has been sick around here. How disgusting and I've trod in it.'

Paying no attention to his comments of discomfort I carried on backfilling the soil. As I looked up the man was frantically trying to remove the contents that he had picked up on his shoe by scraping it across the grass at the same time sounding out exclamations of profanities.

'Well, as you don't want me to help you, I'll be on my way,' said the motorist.

I was relieved when I saw the man return to his car and drive off. I couldn't be sure if this man was suspicious or not, but couldn't take the chance, so I hurriedly finished off and was pleased to get back in the van and move off.

Driving South I headed in the direction of Southampton with all the van windows wide open in an attempt to eradicate the pungent stench of the body which filled the vehicle. Wherever I was going I had to quickly get clear of Guildford for two reasons. Firstly I didn't want my vehicle being identified as being in the Guildford area and secondly the smell of death in the van was rancid and unpleasantly overpowering.

It was now one o'clock in the morning and I had found a wooded area just before reaching the English South Coast. It was here that I decided would be Ralph's final resting place. I briefly looked around to see if there was anyone around. On seeing no one in the immediate vicinity, I commenced work. By this time I was so well acquainted with hole sizes, I was now able to accomplish the dig without the aid of a measuring tape.

Moving the load took all my strength and when I had managed to transfer it to the newly dug hole, I collapsed on the ground with exhaustion. Backfilling soil was equally as tiring. I could only manage a couple of spades of soil at a time, because as this was a public area I needed to constantly look around me to see if anyone was witnessing what I was doing.

When I had finished, I was totally exhausted having done so much hand digging and headed off home thankful that it was now all behind me. I collapsed into bed every muscle in my body aching and although I knew my worries were far from over, drifted off quickly with tiredness into a deep sleep.

One week later one of the national newspapers reported that they had found the body of the murdered wife, the story which Alice was so eager to tell me that dominated the tabloid newspapers. However it was also reported that they had come across another recent excavation in the course of their searches which indicated traces of human remains. It went on to report that samples of these traces had been taken by the police for further analysis. It was also reported that they had taken some urine samples extracted from the stains on a fir tree which they had managed to match up with someone recently discharged from jail who they were currently questioning.

In reading this I was struck with horror, as it was not difficult to come to the realisation that they must have stumbled across my excavation first. I counted myself fortunate that I had acted proactively in moving Ralph. Although I was aware that there was nothing to link me with their findings, it was still nevertheless of concern that the police had now opened another file. There was also the man they were questioning who must have been the same person who interrupted my earthworks. It was questionable whether or not he managed to get a good description of me in the dark, also would he have had the forethought to take my vehicle registration number. I was also horrified that the police had in their custody an innocent man. If they charged this man with a murder, then my conscience would not allow me to send a man to jail for something I had done. If there was any danger that this would be a reality then I would have to approach the police with a full confession.

Also in the same newspaper was a totally unrelated article on a different page about Ralph Brown described as a missing person. I realised that as notification of his apparent absence had now reached the national newspapers, it had become evident that there would be a widespread search.

As the days went by I was having great difficulty in sleeping and whenever I was able to drift off into a deep sleep, nightmares had become a regular occurrence. The only way I was going to get through this was to try and forget the events that had occurred over the last two months and try and lead as normal life as it was possible to do. However given the current circumstances, changing the pattern of my thoughts was going to be extremely difficult, but I had to try.

I began by phoning Alice, started my telephone conversation with an apology for my sudden change in my health and suggested that we go out to dinner again. Alice was very pleased to hear from me and accepted my apology with understanding. She also agreed to the invitation I had put to her.

On the day I had arranged to see Alice, I made up my mind that I would behave myself, by not making any excuses of sudden fake illnesses and not closing the date early, as I had done on the previous one.

We had arranged to meet at the same Indian Restaurant where we had dined before. When I arrived, Alice was already sitting at a table. I greeted Alice with a peck on the cheek and sat down opposite her. Alice looked me up and down and put some questions towards me regarding my health.

'Have you completely recovered?' asked Alice, 'you didn't look at all well the last time I saw you. In fact I thought you were going to pass out.'

'Why was I turning a different colour?' I asked.

'Yes,' admitted Alice, 'you went red and I could see perspiration coming from your brow.'

'I'm, okay,' I replied, keen to get off the subject of my health, 'let's order.'

During the meal Alice was again constantly talking about her favourite topic of conversation, being legal cases.

'I told you. They did find that woman. You know the wife killed by her husband. They also found where she was buried by air surveillance, just as I had predicted,' she said.

'Yes, you were right,' I replied keeping my answers short in order not to extend or go into detail on this topic of conversation to which I had become completely averse.

'What I don't understand,' she continued, 'they also found an empty grave in another field.'

'Yes, very odd,' I replied still keeping my answers short.

'I think this one is baffling the police, but they will uncover this, you mark my words,' said Alice.

'Oh, they may not find anything,' I replied.

'They are also questioning a man who admits being at the scene. I bet he knows more than he is letting on,' commented Alice.

'Look Alice, do you mind if we change the subject,' I requested.

As Alice was working through the theme of what she had read in the newspapers which were dressed up with her own conclusions, I was becoming more and more uncomfortable.

'Not at all,' accepted Alice 'I thought you may have been interested.'

'Well I am interested, but I'll think you'll agree, it's a bit of a distasteful subject to talk about while we are eating,' I insisted.

From then onwards to my utter relief we spoke about our past holidays, buildings of interest, cooking and anything other than past crime and recent crime publicised in the tabloid newspapers. However even though we weren't talking about the empty grave that was found, it was still constantly on my mind.

Chapter 6 Moves in with Alice

It was now two months since the police had discovered the empty grave. The newspapers fortunately had dropped the story surrounding Ralph Brown and also released the man who admitted being in the farmer's field in Guildford. In the time that had passed I found that everything was getting a little easier, even to the extent that I was enjoying life once again. I had been seeing Alice on a regular basis, who from our latest chats had obviously taken the hint that I didn't want any further discussions on crime, prisons or courtroom dramas. However what I had noticed about myself during our discussions since that fateful night, was that I had become a compulsive liar. In order to protect my guilty secret, lies had become an habitual way of life.

One afternoon, Alice had invited me to her house for dinner. I regarded this as something special because I had never been invited to Alice's home before, so I was mystified at what awaited me.

Alice greeted me with a hug and invited me inside the house.

'Please sit in the lounge,' she said 'I'm still preparing dinner.'

I sat down and turned my attention to my immediate surroundings. It appeared that Alice lived very comfortably in a detached house with three bedrooms. The house was full of antique furniture and plaster ornaments. I noticed everywhere was decorated to a tasteful high standard and the inclusion of many plants on tables and window sills complimented the home with a very pleasant ambience and feeling of warmth. The bookshelves were however crammed with legal literature which unmistakably disclosed the profession in which she worked.

Dinner was soon over and we continued the evening chatting over a glass of wine.

'Come on Rick,' she said, 'I have need of you.'

'Really, I'll help if I can,' I replied.

Alice led the way and I followed believing that she wanted me to do a household task. I couldn't have been more wrong. Alice grabbed my hand and started to lead me into the bedroom. I was not sure this was what I wanted, because not only was I out of practice in bedroom sexual activity, but the events over the last couple of months was having a physical setback on my body, particularly in the genital region.

Alice started by peeling off her clothes down to her brassier and knickers and slipped between the sheets on the bed.

It was a long time since I'd seen a female body in the flesh and I must admit from first glances Alice certainly had a well formed body.

'Come on,' she said patting the empty side of the bed 'what are you waiting for?'

I started to disrobe myself down to my pants and was conscious that I was taking my time. Even at that moment I was apprehensive and worried about my probable performance and didn't want to make a fool of myself.

I slowly climbed into the bed still taking my time. When I pulled the bed covers over me, I froze lying on my back looking up at the ceiling. However Alice had brought me into the bedroom for a purpose and she made sure she wasn't going to be disappointed.

'Come on, come over to this side of the bed,' requested Alice. Apprehensively I did as she asked.

'I am still married you know,' I warned.

I made a move to climb out of the bed realising that I had made a big mistake.

Alice saw what I was trying to do and immediately pulled me back. As I hit the pillow, Alice climbed over me, thus preventing any form of escape and started to passionately kiss me.

I then felt her hand slide across my stomach and down my pants. She soon found my penis and started to gently caress it. All my cares and worries were disappearing as she rhythmically ran her hand up and down the length of my member making it elongate and harden in the process. I was now sexually aroused and felt my animal instincts coming into play. With one swift action I had ripped off her knickers and started to return the pleasure by caressing her vagina which had now become wet and open.

I rolled her over on the bed so that I was now in command and teasingly touched the opening of her vagina with my penis, which Alice grabbed hold of and guided it into her body gently. I continued this activity using a rhythmic action on her to heighten the pleasure between us.

While all this was going on I could hear Alice giving moans of delight. It wasn't long before both of us climaxed and we were lying on our backs exhausted in the bed.

After approximately an hour I climbed out of the bed and grabbed some of my clothes ready to put them on.

'What are you doing and where are you going?' asked Alice.

'Home,' I said, 'I'm going home,' I repeated.

'Well you might as well stay here,' replied Alice, 'pick up your belongings from home in the morning and bring them over here. In fact you can stay here for as long as you like.'

This seemed like an invitation requiring some permanency and as I was no longer living with Joy it was something I was content to embrace. I began to think that maybe Alice could make me very happy, so I did not argue with her suggestion. In fact the more I thought about it, the more I was delighted by the idea.

The following day I gave notice of my intention to leave the tenanted property to the Landlord and moved all my belongings into Alice's house.

Alice and I had now lived together for a full ten months and in that time it appeared that Alice and I were getting on extremely well in a relationship of mutual compatibility. However in finding complete happiness, the guilty secret I was carrying was beginning to take its toll on me again and all the old worries started to return. I was aware that I would never get rid of these bad feelings unless I was honest with Alice and confessed to her what I had done.

I picked my moment and waited until Alice was in a good mood, which fortunately for me was most of the time. When the moment came for me to reveal all, I was a bag of nerves and stuttered my way through the opening sentences of my confession.

'Alice, it is important that I tell you something which could ultimately affect our relationship,' I said.

'You look extremely serious and nervous. Listen I don't think that there is anything that could affect our relationship,' she replied as she put her hand on mine and putting me at my ease.

I started to relate to Alice the problem that had been plaguing my mind wondering all the time how she would take it. Holding nothing back I told Alice the whole sorry experience regarding the stabbing of Ralph Brown, moving the body twice, together with all my concerns. Alice listened intently and never said a word until I had finished.

'I often wondered why from time to time you looked as if you were in a world of your own, and do you mean to say that it was me that alerted you to move Brown's body to Southampton,' Alice observed.

'Yes, it was,' I admitted.

'Is that the reason why you have wandered off and taken walks to be on your own?' asked Alice.

'Well, it hasn't been easy for me and I felt that as our relationship has moved on, I didn't want to keep any secrets from you,' I confessed. 'I must say I feel a lot better now that I have got it off my chest. It's like I've unloaded a heavy weight off my mind,'

I was aware after I had confessed everything to Alice, her mood had suddenly changed and I noticed that she had removed her hand from mine and looked a bit more serious. I was desperate to know how she felt about what I had told her and after a long uncomfortable pause I listened to the words I didn't want her to say.

'You are aware that I will have to report what you have just told me to the police,' Alice said.

'What? Why would you want to do that?' I asked in a concerned and startled manner. 'I thought we were getting on. I thought that there was something special between us.'

'Rick you are right there is something special between us, but you know it is my profession and duty to uphold the law. How can I do that when I am concealing the details of a crime to which you have just confessed and to which I am now very much aware?' said Alice.

'Look Alice, I told you this in the utmost confidence. If I thought you were going to reveal what I have just told you to the police, then I would never have mentioned it to you. They will throw the book at me for this, and I couldn't face prison again,' I urged.

'I'm sorry, I can see no alternative,' replied Alice. As she finished her sentence she burst into tears. I did all I could to console her by hugging her close to me.

'Is there nothing you can do to help me?' I asked.

Alice thought long and hard and it was some time before I received an answer, which again was contrary to my liking.

'You must go to the police and tell them everything you have told me,' requested Alice.

'Sorry Alice, I can not do that and I won't do that,' I said dogmatically.

'Then you are stupid. Look, if you are totally against going to the police, I will tell you what to do,' sobbed Alice.

'Gather up as many of your belongings as you can carry and leave here immediately. For my part I have no alternative, I will still have to inform the police everything I know. However, I won't tell them anything until three hours have elapsed after you have left here. I'll explain to them that I tried to inform them earlier but had a problem with my phone,' said a tearful Alice.

In a way I could understand Alice's predicament and although unpalatable, I followed her instructions and left her house. I walked down her path opened the gate and looked back. I left Alice waving me goodbye, clearly upset by my leaving and my revelation.

I continued walking and heard Alice gently close the door after I had disappeared from her view. I looked behind, hoping that Alice would have changed her mind and come after me. My wishes were not satisfied and I realised that once again I was on my own.

I was sure that Alice would keep to her word in giving me the three hours grace to make my escape, but I wasn't certain how I was going to take advantage of this short moratorium or where I was going to go. All I knew was that I had to make the most of the time Alice had allowed me. I got in my car and headed off at speed.

Chapter 7 On the Run

It now seemed essential that in order to stay out of prison I had to make an escape and thought that it would be more difficult for the police to find me if I moved out of the country. I headed towards the Port of Dover believing that if I caught a ferry to France, I would be at least out of the British Isles. However, would I make it in the three hours Alice had allowed me? It was going to be tight and a test of my driving ability.

I arrived at the Port of Dover ten minutes ahead of my scheduled time and waited my turn to go through customs behind a long line of cars. I noticed that the next ship to leave the port was in forty five minutes allowing me plenty of time to catch this ferry. However it was essential that I get through customs in the ten minutes I had allowed myself.

The queue of cars in front of me moved very slowly, and I could see that I wasn't going to be allowed to pass the mandatory regulative checking point within the crucial time. In fact a full half hour had elapsed from the time I had joined the queue to the time I had reached the passport official.

On request I nervously handed over my documents to the checker. He looked at the passport, then looked at me, then looked at the passport again. By this time my body was running hot and cold waiting for the return of my documents.

'Please wait here for a moment,' said the official still retaining my personal documents.

I noticed through the window in his cabin, that he had left his seat to pick up a telephone. My immediate thoughts were that I had been rumbled, although I couldn't be certain, but I wasn't going to take the chance.

Looking in my car mirror I noticed that there was a large gap between me and the next car, sufficient to reverse, turn and make my escape. With a screech of tyres and plenty of acceleration I managed to turn the car around and head of in the direction that I had come, albeit in a prohibited direction against the flow of traffic. An official saw that I was heading in the wrong way and tried to flag me down. Swerving the car I managed to steer clear of him, but noticed in my rear view mirror that he was taking the number of my car. With a bit more acceleration and erratic driving, I succeeded in getting clear of the port.

My mind was in turmoil although my brain kept telling me that I had to get out of the country and without a passport. That was not going to be easy. The only way I was going to do it was to buy a boat.

I approached a chandler and boat yard in Dover. Within minutes a middle aged man approached me and asked if he could help.

'Yes, I have been looking at this boat. Do you think it is seaworthy?' I enquired.

'No,' he said, 'this one is only for river sailing,' he assured.

'Why, only fit for river sailing? I asked.

'That's because it has got a hole in the bottom, so that if you are on the river and it sinks you haven't got that far to swim to a river bank,' he answered.

In different circumstances I may have chuckled at this funny remark, but I was in no mood for jokes and asked him if he had a similar boat but seaworthy.

'I've got this one,' he said, 'I can let you have it for six hundred pounds,' he said.

'Yes, but is it seaworthy,' I insisted.

'Seaworthy? You could sail round the world in this,' he replied.

After a careful check of the fibreglass hull and sails, I made an offer to the overzealous salesman of five hundred pounds. The next thing I knew, I was the proud owner of a boat which I treated with absolute care when I launched into the water. With a solid push, an energetic leap into the craft and a hoist of the sail I was on my way waving England a fond farewell.

The boat appeared seaworthy, but I was conscious that it was too small to cater for very rough seas. Fortunately for me the sea was reasonably calm, around force one to two in strength. Although this helped my craft to sustain a more stable consistency in the water, the light winds became a disadvantage. This was because I needed the stronger winds to move me quicker through the water and keep me on course. Although I wasn't an ardent sailor I had experienced using wind assisted vessels before, so I knew the rudiments of tacking against the wind and when conditions required the use of a spinnaker sail.

After one hour I could still see the white cliffs of Dover as if they were only yards away. When two hours had elapsed I seemed to be making a bit more headway but the seas were roughing up a bit and had reached a strength of between forces three and four. It was noticeable also that I was taking in a bit of water. When I hit the three hour mark I was approximately halfway across the English Channel but the extra water I was taking on board was slowing me down badly and whilst tacking the sail I was also frantically bailing out water with a small bucket. When I had been travelling four hours the sea had calmed down again and I was about four hundred yards off the French coast. Even though I was so tantalisingly close, at this point I didn't appear to be making any headway and a strong current appeared to be taking me South, but frustratingly not any closer to the beaches of France.

I had now been in the water five hours and my predicament was getting worse. The current had drifted me off course further south and away from the French coast till it was almost out of site and to add to my problems I was taking in water again and the wind was building up. I looked at the sun which was dropping over the horizon telling me that it wouldn't be long before it had completely disappeared and nightfall would be upon me. It was then I felt fearful for my life and started to panic. Looking hopelessly at the water around me lapping at the sides of my drifting boat, not knowing what to do next, I continued to bale out water.

There were two oars in the boat which I connected up to some rowlocks. Pulling at the oars I managed to turn the boat into the direction of the coast and continued rowing. After thirty minutes I could see the futility of my efforts, because I had made no headway against the current at all. If anything I was drifting backwards. This was a serious setback as I was now running out of options.

I took down my sail as this didn't appear to be helping me at all and continued baling water out of the boat. The craft was by this time quite low in the sea making it easier for the water to come crashing over the bow and into the boat. Water entering the boat was more than I was able to extract so I knew it wouldn't be long before the vessel would give up to the seas with me in it and I was aware that if I ended up in the water, then my fate would be completely sealed.

I was at the point of completely giving up, when to my surprise I saw a motorboat powering through the water in the distance. Frantically I started waving my arms and shouting to gain some attention. The motorboat had obviously seen my distress signal, because to my relief it changed course and headed in my direction. As it got closer the day was getting darker and when the craft finally arrived to my rescue, it was pitch black in darkness.

'What's the matter mate, you seem to be drifting off course,' the concerned seaman enquired.

I was delighted that the man spoke English. If he had been French or Spanish I might have had some linguistic problems and unable to talk my way out of my problem.

'Oh, I afraid I've got myself into a spot of bother,' I said in embarrassment.

'Do you want a tow to the coast,' asked the seaman looking down at me and shaking his head in disbelief at all the water in the craft.

'I would be most grateful to receive your help,' I replied.

In the darkness I was just about able to pick this man out as being around fifty five years old, stocky in appearance with a cheery face, full beard and moustache.

'First we had better get some of that water out of your boat,' said the seaman as he shone his torch into the bottom of the craft. He then placed a water pump in the base of the hull and within minutes the boat was no longer an unstable paddling pool but a vessel that bobbed up and down in the water once again. The acceptance of a tow rope saw us on our way cutting through the waves. In order to give my craft a bit of assisted direction I opted to stay in the towed craft.

After two and a half hours on tow I was thrilled to see the coast against a dimly lit moon. The motorboat gently pulled me in up the beach for which I heaped appreciation on my helper. I dragged my small sailing boat up the beach and looked around me. I couldn't believe my eyes, for in the darkness I could just make out the unmistakable outline of the white cliffs. I wasn't in France at all I was back where I started in Dover.

I called out to the man who saved me from the fate of possible drowning and the elements.

'I thought you were going to take me to the coast,' I said.

'This is the coast,' he replied.

'I meant the French coast,' I said now frustrated by his naivety.

'Well you didn't say the French coast when I picked you up and I after all was heading this way,' he replied.

Although I was grateful to be alive I was nevertheless furious that I had spent the last eight hours on the sea and finished where I'd started. As I dragged the boat up the beach, I noticed two men walking towards me and the good Samaritan who helped me. By the time they had reached us he was reversing the motorboat back into the water.

'Not so fast, bring it back in,' demanded one of the men.

The motorboat owner did as he was told.

One of the men reached into his pocket and pulled out an official looking card and held it up for display.

'Customs and Excise,' one of them said as they introduced themselves.

As the officials seemed to be addressing the motorboat owner I started to walk off to retrieve my trailer.

'And where do you think you are going?' asked one of the officials.

I looked behind me, noticed that he was talking to me and stopped in my tracks.

'We have had our surveillance equipment on you both and noticed that the two of you have come from the direction of France. We must therefore inspect your vessels to see if you are carrying drugs or anything contraband,' informed the official.

'Sure, would you like to inspect me first?' I asked.

The official didn't answer but clambered into my sailing boat with a torch and made a thorough search. Meanwhile the other official began searching the motorboat.

'This one is clean,' he said as he climbed out of my sailing vessel.

Again I started to walk off to retrieve my trailer and again I was ordered to return back.

'We haven't finished yet, my colleague is still checking the other craft belonging to your friend,' the official said.

I waited until the other Custom's official had finished his search on the motorboat.

'I've found something here,' he said, 'it looks to be amphetamines.'

Heaving a sigh of despair and I wondered how long it would be before they detected that I was a person the run.   I looked at the motorboat owner who had remained silent throughout the whole process.

'I'm afraid we will have to hold the two of you for further questioning,' said one of the officials.

'Look,' I protested, 'I don't even know this man.   He kindly gave me a tow when he saw that I was in trouble.'

'Is that right?' said the official directing the question to the motorboat owner.

'Yes, he has told you the truth,' he confirmed.

'Alright then you and only you are free to go,' said the official.   He turned to the drug suspect, 'but you will remain here.'

Having been cleared by the Customs officials, I took the opportunity to go. However I noticed during the search on my property that luckily they hadn't asked me my name.

I winched the boat on its trailer and managed to clear myself of the beach,   I looked up and could see my car. I was amazed that it hadn't been stolen, after all I had left the keys in the ignition with thoughts that my boat trip was only going to be one way and therefore would have no need for the vehicle any more, thinking that it would be left for the benefit of an opportunist thief.

Tired with every muscle of my body aching, I opened my car door climbed inside, made myself comfortable and dropped off into a deep sleep. The next day I was woken by the sun streaming through the car rear window. I was aware following my disastrous results in sailing, the first task I had to do was to rid myself of the boat that had taken me on a fool's errand. I took the boat back to the boatyard where I had made the sale and asked them if they wanted to buy it back.

The same man who sold it to me looked all round it carefully, scrutinised the hull as if he'd never seen the craft before, shook his head and started to walk away displaying an obvious, but tactful lack of interest.

'Aren't you interested in buying it back?' I asked.

'It's in very poor condition so it's not worth very much,' he replied.

'That's not what you said when you sold it to me, in fact you told me that I could sail the world in it,' I argued.

'The problem is that its poor condition doesn't make it seaworthy,' he pointed out.

'Again that's not what you told me when you sold it to me,' I argued.

'Look, I'll give you fifty pounds for it and that's my final offer,' he said.

I was stunned by his change of attitude regarding the value of the craft, his signs of disinterest and low offer made to me by this rogue of a boat chandler.

'That's daylight robbery, I gave you five hundred pounds when I bought it yesterday,' I insisted.

'Take it or leave it,' he said in an uncaring manner as he started to walk away.

My circumstances dictated that I couldn't roam the country in a car towing a boat and drawing attention to myself, I would be immediately recognised and picked up. I therefore had no alternative than to accept his derisory offer. My futile attempt in escaping the police had resulted in a trip to France and back, with the loss of four hundred and fifty pounds. Under different situations, I would have seen the funny side of my ineptitudes and misfortunes, but this was a dilemma I had placed myself in and had to be treated with the seriousness of the occasion. Nevertheless I couldn't dwell on my mistakes, I had to think positively. I started the car and headed out of Dover taking the coast road.

Chapter 8 Finding Somewhere to Stay

Having driven for a while I noticed a sign indicating a direction towards Hastings and then another sign with the word 'Campsite' on it. Quickly weighing up the pros and cons I decided that staying at a campsite would probably solve my problem of accommodation. However I needed some essential camping equipment, tent, sleeping bag, cooking stove, water carrier and the like.   I drove into Hastings, found myself a camping shop and purchased these essential items, then drove out of the town back to where I had seen the camping sign.

As I approached the camping office I put on a hat and concealed my face partly with a handkerchief by pretending that I had an awful cold. I opened the door and walked in keeping up the pretence that I was sick with the fever of a cold.

'You sound dreadful,' said the warden, 'don't come too near me, I don't want to catch it.'

The warden was a middle aged man and called himself Donald Evans. He had ginger hair with a ginger moustache and was approximately five feet nine inches in height.

'I'd like to make a booking for a week,' I informed him.

'Give me your name and address and I'd like to know if you have a caravan, mobile camper or a tent,' said Evans.

'My name is Richard and I paused and started coughing while I thought of a suitable false name. 'Blake' I said when I had decided on a name. Richard Blake I reiterated. I am currently between buying properties at the moment, that is why I need to stay here, also in answer to your last question, I own a tent,' I informed him, still partly covering my face with the handkerchief and coughing into it.

'Right, that will be seventy pounds and you can pick any pitch that you would like except those that are supplied with electricity. Now remove yourself from this office quickly Mr. Blake because I don't wish to be catching your cold,' he demanded.

I was thankful to follow his instructions and soon found myself a suitable pitch close to a hedge of small trees, and commenced erecting my tent. In exploring the site I noticed that there were no other campers on the site which suited me fine. It was after all mid November and the camping season was coming to an end. I was aware that I couldn't stay on the site for ever because there would be a time when it would close down for the winter and I would be asked to leave. However it suited my purposes for the time being and I resigned myself for a temporary lonely life under canvas.

Having erected my tent and loaded all my equipment into it, I went off to explore the washing facilities on the site. These were clean but very basic, with four showers and four W.C. cubicles. The water point was close to my pitch as was the rubbish skip.

As night came I climbed into my sleeping bag ready for a good night's slumber. I had just fallen asleep when I was awakened by car headlights streaming through the canvas of my tent. Then there was a lot of activity going on close by. I peered through a slit in the door opening and saw a man and a woman putting up an awning on the side of a caravan in the next pitch to me, which must have been only twelve feet from where my tent was erected.

As I knew that my current circumstances demanded absolute privacy, I was devastated that they had chosen to set up camp next to me when they had the choice of the whole campsite at their disposal.

I was tired and therefore didn't dwell on it for too long and was soon back to sleep.

In the morning, I was woken to the smell of a fried breakfast coming from the adjacent pitch. The constant sizzling of fat and the aroma of bacon coming from the caravan made me want to get my own stove going with food in a frying pan. The only problem was that being in a tent I had to prepare anything I cooked outside in the open air in full view of everyone.

As I ventured out of the tent I was greeted with a friendly 'hello' from my neighbour who was a middle aged man with grey hair and approximately five feet ten inches in height. The last thing I wanted to do was to get it to conversation with this man, but it looked as though my wishes were not going to be granted because he walked over to me and started to engage in conversation.

'My name is Terry, who are you?'

'I'm Richard,' I said, trying to keep my answers as short as possible.

'Nice to meet you Richard,' he replied extending his hand for a handshake.

'Where do you come from?' he asked.

'Dover,' I replied still not wishing to progress the conversation with him.

'Did you see the news on the television last night?' he asked.

'No, I didn't,' I replied.

'Well, they were reporting a man that had killed a teenager who is on the run from the police,' he said.

My ears pricked up at this snippet of the national news that my camping neighbour had recently heard.

'Did they give the name of this murderer on the television?' I asked.

'Yes, they did, but I can't recall what it was now. They didn't even disclose a picture of him, but they did show a photograph of the victim with his sister,' said Terry.

I was relieved that my picture had not been emblazoned on every television in the country, but was aware that it wouldn't be long before my photograph would be the subject of media attention.

'No I can confirm that I didn't see it,' I answered, hoping my visitor would retrace his steps back to his caravan.

'Yes, the news covering requested that the public be vigilante and report anything they know,' said Terry.

At that moment I was relieved when Terry's wife called out to him.

'Terry, your breakfast is ready.'

'Coming my sweetness and light,' he called back.

'Nice meeting you Richard, I'll see you later,' said Terry.

With that response he was gone, leaving me to continue cooking my breakfast.

After breakfast I went along to the communal ablutions to have a shower, only to find Terry in there having a wash.

'Hello again,' he said.

'Oh hello Terry,' I answered heading towards the shower cubicles.

'How long are you staying on this campsite?' he asked.

My realisation that Terry, who just wanted to be friendly but was now becoming a nosy nuisance with his questions, finally decided that I had to change my plans. Although I had booked my pitch on the campsite for a week it was becoming more awkward to remain there another day.

'I have decided that I will be leaving as soon as I have had a shower,' I told Terry.

I started to feel uncomfortable with Terry acting like a constant shadow over me, and couldn't wait to have my shower and get clear of the campsite. When I arrived back at my tent, I immediately started to dismantle it by pulling up the tent pegs only to find that Terry had wandered over to help me. His assistance was not something that I wanted and I tried politely to inform him that I didn't need his help, but he was most insistent, the experience fraught with many questions about myself.

When I went into the warden's office to say I was leaving and request the return of some money for my shortened stay, he was keen to ask me a few questions.

'Mr. Evans I wish to leave today,' I advised.

'Richard Blake, isn't it?' asked the warden.

'Yes that's right,' I replied.

'You arrived here yesterday with a nasty cold. It seems to be a lot better today,' said the warden.

'Yes, I appear to have recovered,' I replied.

'I see you have booked for a week, so why do you want to rush off early? Don't you like the campsite?' asked the warden.

'Yes, the campsite is fine but I have to rush off due to personal reasons,' I replied.

'You know, you remind me of someone, but I can't place who,' said the warden desperately trying to recall his memory, 'I know it's that man the police are trying to find. You know, the one that killed a teenager. You look just like him. His name was also Richard.'

'I think I know who you mean, I do look a little bit like him although, he has a slightly longer nose than me and a little bit taller,' I replied.

The warden's recognition that there was a fugitive who looked exactly like me set my pulse racing and my body trembling. I wasn't sure whether or not he was convinced that I was that person.

'No, you can't have a refund, because in reserving you a pitch for a week, you have prevented me from taking another booking for the pitch that you occupied,' explained the warden.

As the campsite was virtually empty I could not accept the warden's explanation for withholding my money, but as he had pointed out to me a similarity between a fugitive and myself, I was in no position to argue with him. I therefore accepted his point and quickly left his office.

As I walked to my car there was a realisation that wherever I went, I could be recognised and this situation would remain until time or circumstance eradicated the image of my face from the memories of the general public.

Back on the road I continued towards Hastings.

*

Continuing along the coast road, I stopped at a bed and breakfast Guest House in Hastings, where I booked myself in for staying the night and possibly longer. The accommodation was very basic, but good enough for someone like me who wanted something reasonably comfortable but wasn't looking for niceties of social living.

In the morning I came down the staircase, heading towards the dining room. As I walked through the hallway I heard the letter box rattle with the delivery of the morning papers. I immediately retrieved them, quickly looking through all the pages.

I couldn't believe it when I saw my picture on the front page of one of the tabloid newspapers, with the heading 'Have you seen this man?' I read the contents under the heading which said:-

> *'Richard Wallace aged 35 is on the run after having killed Ralph Brown. He is approximately six feet in height with jet black hair. It is believed he is somewhere hiding in Great Britain possibly in the South of England, last seen in the port of Dover yesterday afternoon. This man is dangerous and should not in any circumstances be approached.'*

Dropping the newspapers on the mat where I had retrieved them, I decided that I had read enough of the article. The tabloids appeared to portray me as some absolute hard line gangster. Foregoing breakfast I immediately paid my lodging account, left the Guest House and made for my car. Now I really and truly did not know what to do or where I was going next. I was indeed a marked man on the run and speculated that I could easily be recognised wherever I went.

*

I wasn't sure where I was heading but just continued driving following the coast at the south of the country, then I saw a town boundary sign which read 'Bournemouth'. I put on the car brakes when I saw some lit up buildings and noticed that I had stopped outside a bed and breakfast Guest House, whereupon I decided I would investigate with a view to rest for the night. A Mrs Janice Knight, the proprietor, answered the door and I was duly invited in. She was a slim kindly lady approximately fifty five years of age, dark curly hair and very pale complexion.

'I'd like to stay here for a few nights,' I told her at the same time purposely giving her a false name of Richard Blake.

'Of course,' she answered, I have plenty of room. After two days of Mrs Knight's hospitality I could confirm she was right about low accommodation, because I was the only one staying there. The lack of residents I considered to be my good fortune because there was no one around to recognise me. Mrs Knight who preferred to be called Janice was a friendly person and in the space of a week we had been getting on very well together. Such was the enjoyment of her gregarious company, I felt that I had known her all my life.

In the course of our conversations, I began to ask her about her private life.

'I notice you live alone here. Do you have a husband?' I asked.

'Well I did until six months ago, until he moved in with a younger woman,' Janice replied.

'Oh, I'm indeed sorry to hear that,' I said sympathetically.

'Don't worry I've become used to being alone, in fact I'm now beginning to enjoy my solitary existence, and if I am truthful I'm not sorry that he has gone,' said Janice.

As time passed I was quite enjoying my time at my new found address and had no immediate plans to move on. The beach was close by and I would often go for walks. However if I ventured outside I had to make sure that my face was partially covered because I didn't want to be recognised by anyone who had seen my picture in the newspaper. Then one morning at breakfast, I noticed a sudden change in Janice's attitude towards me. Her mannerisms were completely unusually hostile towards me and began thinking that I had upset her in some way. This was the last thing I wanted to do particularly as I had found an accommodation that I liked and had settled in quite comfortably.

'Is anything troubling you?' I asked Janice, 'You don't seem your usual cheery self.'

'More to the point is anything troubling you?' she replied turning the question back on me.

'I prefer to keep my troubles to myself,' I answered.

'I bet you do. You are not Richard Blake, are you? You have lied about your name,' she quizzed, 'you are Richard Wallace aren't you. The one in the newspaper, the one police are looking for. Yet you don't appear to be a cold blooded murderer.'

I looked up at Janice who appeared attentive obviously waiting for an answer. Realising how good she had been to me since arriving I couldn't lie to her.

'Yes, you are right, Blake is not my name, neither am I a murderer, although I did kill someone who had a strangle hold on my wife,' I answered nervously in agreement.

'I knew I couldn't be wrong. You are a fool Rick you should have told me earlier. You do realise that you have put me in a difficult position,' she said.

'What are you going to do, now that you know? Are you going to call the police?' I asked as my voice wavered nervously.

'That depends on you,' she said, 'tell me your side of the story, what you did, why you did it and more importantly why you are running away from the police.'

I told her exactly what I had told Alice and when I'd finished, convinced myself that her attitude was going to be the same as Alice's, with similar disastrous consequences and braced myself for the moment of disappointment. However when I'd completed the story of my woeful experiences in all its full horror, I was rather surprised by her unexpected reaction.

'Look,' she said, 'I will not turn informer on you. I will not tell anyone what you have told me, and as far as I am concerned you can stay here for as long as you like. However you must promise me that if things get a little difficult around here, you will not embarrass me by staying.'

I thanked Janice, confirmed her requests and heaved a sigh of relief that it had not been more serious. I was also pleased that she still saw me as just one of the usual guests that she gets calling on her.

From then onwards everything was the same as before I had revealed to Janice the events of that awful night. Also I felt I had found a true friend whom I could trust. When I told Janice that I had worked in the building industry she made use of my disclosure by taking the opportunity to make me do running repairs around the Guest House and even paid me for doing the work. In helping each other, it was a great relationship which had developed and I was more than happy to give Janice's residence some form of permanency.

Two months after my full revelation disclosure to Janice, a young married couple called at the Guest House who wanted to stay for two nights. Naturally, Janice was glad of the business, but it did create a problem for me, particularly as I had been used to being Janice's sole resident, but I was aware I had also become the subject of media attention. I asked Janice about the time scales she had given her guests for breakfast and suggested having mine thirty minutes earlier, so that my meal did not clash chronologically with theirs. Janice kindly obliged.

The next day I was enjoying breakfast alone and reading the newspaper, when Janice's two young guests entered the dining room. They had obviously come into breakfast before the scheduled times given to them by Janice. They were very loving and tactile towards each other and so wrapped up in each others company that I was sure they wouldn't notice me at the other end of the dining room. Then just as I was feeling secure in my own company, the man started to speak to me.

'Good morning, nice day and I see its stopped raining,' said the man, 'anything interesting in the paper?'

I quickly scanned the pages and was relieved to see that there was nothing in there which was remotely connected to me.

'Oh, nothing but the usual rubbish, I don't know why I bother to read it,' I replied. 'Here would you like to have a look? I've finished with it.'

Immediately I began feeling uncomfortable and started to vacate the table, leaving behind a half finished fried breakfast. As I opened the dining room door to leave, I noticed the woman lean across to the man and whisper in his ear. I didn't hear what she said and I didn't know if she recognised me, after all, my photograph had been emblazoned on the front pages of the tabloid newspapers, but her body language was enough for me to be suspicious and whether or not I was correct in my assumptions, I couldn't take the chance. As I was about to leave the room, the young woman turned her body and looked at me.

'Just a minute, I do believe I know you,' she said.

'No, I think you must be mistaken,' I insisted almost before she finished her sentence.

'No,' she said, 'I never forget a face. You are the one that saved my life on that day in June. I remember you putting a tourniquet on my leg to stop the bleeding.'

'Now I know you are definitely mistaken,' I again insisted.

This young woman's recognition of me doing a noble deed had resurrected a new set of problems, because she appeared to be astute in her remembrance of faces. A connection between her saviour and the killer of a teenager as reported in the newspapers could easily be made by someone so competent. In order to prevent any further follow-up questions from this lady, I left the dining room.

Against my wishes I did the only thing I could do under the circumstances of being detected, which was collect my meagre belongings, vacate my room and make myself ready to make a run for it.

Seeking out Janice I informed her that I could no longer stay at the Guest House and asked her to quickly make up my final bill. Janice seemed disappointed I was leaving, but I did tell her that I would be back when the focus of attention on me had receded.

Heading out of Bournemouth I noticed in the rear view mirror that there was a police car behind me with the lights on the vehicle's roof flashing. I thought to myself *'don't panic, it's probably nothing, they may not even be after me.'*

I pulled further over to the left of the road, in order to allow the police vehicle to pass me, but expressed horror when the officer signalled me with his hand to stop while he was overtaking.

Shaking all over I obeyed his instructions, as I did not want to draw attention to myself.

The officer left his car and slowly walked over to me. By this time I was a complete bag of nerves although outwardly I had to show calmness.

'Did you know that one of your brake lights is not working, the one on the passenger side,' said the officer.

'No, I wasn't aware,' I replied, relieved he had only stopped me for a minor offence.

'Can I see your driver's licence?' asked the officer.

The driving licence I had in my pocket, but it would have been foolhardy of me to disclose who I was.

'No I'm sorry but I don't have it with me,' I answered.

'Your face looks familiar,' remarked the officer.

'Oh, I been mistaken for many people,' I replied feeling a cold sweat run down my back at my unease in his question.

The officer then put his hand on my chin and turned my face so that I was facing him square on.

'Just a minute, I thought so. I recognise you as being one of those we are looking for,' challenged the officer.

I was dumbstruck. I had been recognised by a traffic cop.

'Can you please give me your name,' insisted the officer.

'Richard Wallace,' I replied, knowing that once I had offered my name, my problems were about to begin.

'I thought as much, the force has been looking for you for some time. Please step out of your car Sir and raise your hands in the air,' said the officer. I did as he asked only to find that after a brief frisking of my person, handcuffs were clamped on me soon after I stepped onto the highway. The cuffs were uncomfortable being secured to my wrists behind my back and every time I moved they would cut into the wrist.

The officer rang a number on his mobile phone saying 'I have just apprehended a suspect and require further backup.' By this time I was trembling all over from the cold air and the realisation that I had been captured, plus I had a pretty good idea what lay ahead of me.

Within a few minutes another police officer arrived and removed my car. I was then taken to a police station where I spent the night in a cell which was open to drafts from several directions. It was not exactly the comfort I had been used to at the Guest House, but better than the comfort I experienced sleeping in my car at Dover.

The following morning I was driven to Scotland Yard headquarters in London, where I was about to be subjected to some in-depth investigation of my movements over the last few days. I was then cautioned and asked if I wanted a legal representative present during the questioning surrounding Ralph Brown's death.

'I would like a solicitor present,' I replied. I thought that the best person to represent me would be Alice, as she now had the knowledge of what had happened on that fateful day. Alice was surprised to hear my voice at the other end of the phone and began her reply by asking if I was alright.

I explained the circumstances which had evolved since I last saw her, conveniently missing out the embarrassing incident with the boat. I didn't want to broadcast my act of maritime stupidity to anyone and thought that was one secret I could keep to myself. Thankfully she agreed to come to the police headquarters and assist me with the police interrogation.

Approximately two hours went by and Alice turned up and we were left in a room on our own.

'Look Alice, I'm terrified about returning to jail. I don't think I can do it,' I said nervously.

Alice ignored my concerns for being in prison again, I think she realised that whatever happened it was going to be unavoidable.

'Rick, you will have to tell them everything that has happened and you will have to tell them the truth,' urged Alice as she put her hand over mine. In this small gesture I could tell that she still had feelings for me as I did for her.

'But I will get life for this. It was because of the repercussions of my actions, that I chose to go on the run,' I replied.

'Well I do think you will be put away for a time, but I can't say how long that will be. That will be up to the judge to decide, but I will warn you that your attempt at escape will definitely not help you,' said Alice.

'I realise now that in some aspects, I have been very silly by letting my fear of jail dictate my actions,' I said sombrely.

'Come on,' said Alice, 'it is time we faced our interrogators. Don't worry, I won't let you answer a question if I thought the response could be damaging or taken out of context.'

Alice knocked on the door and two men walked in. One of the detectives was around the age of forty five years and the other was slightly younger, approximately thirty five. They introduced themselves and attempted to put me at my ease.

'Hello, I am detective inspector Randall and this is detective inspector Littlewood. I have to inform you that this interview will be taped and you will be expected to sign a report based entirely on our discussions. Describe to us in your own words the events on the day Ralph Brown entered your house. We are looking for the circumstances that led up to Ralph Brown's death and subsequently the events that you were involved in after his death,' said Randall.

What they were asking was everything from the time I heard the intruder enter the house to the time I buried Brown for the second time. I told them all I knew, this being the same sorry story I had related to Alice and Janice. In fact I had become so accomplished in relating my experiences of that period in my life that I was able to tell it with oratory perfection indicating dates and times without the aid of reference documents.

'Why, did you stab Brown in the back, after all he was unarmed?' said Littlewood.

'I didn't know that at the time and within the split second when I noticed Brown strangling my wife, I wasn't prepared to waste time finding out whether he was armed or not. He did have his back to me so I was in no position to find out if he had a weapon,' I explained.

'Yes, but if you saw both Brown's hands around your wife's neck, he couldn't have been holding a weapon,' Littlewood pointed out.

'That is true, but he may have had a gun or a knife somewhere else on his body which was not in my range of vision,' I replied.

'When you had discovered that Brown was dead, why didn't you contact the police?' asked Littlewood.

After Littlewood's question, Alice interjected.

'I refuse to let my client answer that question on the grounds that he could be incriminated.

'Where did you finally bury the body?' asked Littlewood.

'Oh, in a wooded area just outside Southampton,' I replied.

'Can you identify the exact place where you buried him?' pressed Littlewood.

'I believe I can,' I answered with certainty.

'Tomorrow, you will be picked up and it will be up to you to take us to the site where the body is buried. It will be in your interest if we can rely on your complete co-operation,' Littlewood pointed out.

'In that case I will help where I can,' I replied as I offered my complete assistance. I noticed that all the fear and anxiety started to come back as I was answering the questions and the trip to Southampton was not something to which I was looking forward.

'I'm afraid we will have to hold you on remand until your court case comes up. It will then be up to the Judge to seal your impending punishment after a Jury has come up with a verdict,' confirmed Randall.

Randall had thrown another unknown to me which added to my concerns.

The following day I was picked up as Littlewood had stated and driven under my guidance, to the wooded area where Ralph was buried and asked to identify the exact location where excavation should commence.

I pointed out the location where I thought the body was interred. The police officers then enclosed the area in a canvas cordon away from public gaze and the digging started. Approximately one hour later and four feet into the hole, I noticed the familiar blue diamond carpet which I had seen so many times before and was the subject of my nightmares. Yes, they had found everything that they were looking for in all its full horror.

'Okay, we've found him,' I heard one of the officers say.

I looked away not wishing to expose my eyes to any more gruesome sites, beyond those I had already witnessed. The next thing I knew was that the body and carpet were being removed in a separate van and I was being driven back to my cell.

Chapter 9 In Court

Three weeks after being picked up I found myself in court. The Court House was packed. Looking around the court, I saw Peter and Dianne Brown who never took their eyes off me when I entered the courthouse. Alice had found a barrister by the name of John Cleaver to defend me in the trial, the outcome of which was to be determined by a jury. I was defending a murder charge. The prosecution for the Crown was represented by a lawyer called David Wilkins.

I was first to go in the dock, whereby I confirmed my name and was made to swear in on the bible, my intention to tell the truth. I was then asked how I pleaded to the charge of murder.

'Not guilty,' I announced as the sound of my voice reverberated around the court.

I was then asked to relate in my own words, the events of that fateful night. Nervously I complied, relating everything I could remember.

Cleaver, my defence was the first to put questions to me.

'When you came from the kitchen into the lounge and saw Brown attacking your wife, did you think he was going to kill her?' asked Cleaver.

'I did,' I answered.

'Did you feel that you had to act in her defence quickly?' asked Cleaver.

'Yes I did,' I replied.

'What was Brown doing to make you feel that you had to act in her defence with such rapidity?' persisted Cleaver.

'He had his hands clasped around Joy's neck as if he was trying to strangle her,' I answered.

'What was your first reaction?' asked Cleaver.

'I tried to pull him off with my hands, but that didn't seem to have any effect, Brown still had his hands around my wife's neck,' I answered.

'After that proved unsatisfactory, what else did you do?' enquired Cleaver.

'I stabbed him in the back, although I did not think that I had put too much pressure on the knife,' I replied.

'Did you feel that stabbing Brown in the back was the only avoiding action you could have taken?' asked Cleaver.

'Well I had to think quickly, to prevent Brown killing Joy, so I suppose the answer must be yes,' I replied.

'Thank you, no further questions,' said Cleaver who then sat down.

I congratulated myself that I had answered the questions put to me by Cleaver reasonably well. Up till then everything was going fine. Then David Wilkins for the prosecution rose to his feet.

'After you had plunged a knife into the back of Brown, what medical help did you receive for yourself and your wife,' asked Wilkins.

'None,' I answered.

'Why did you not seek medical help? After all you had been attacked viciously,' asked Wilkins.

'Well, my wife was the only one that had been attacked by Brown, and she had not sustained any physical damage,' I replied.

'So if you did not have any damage inflicted on you by Brown, why did you feel it necessary to kill him?' persisted Wilkins.

'I wasn't trying to kill him, I was only trying to prevent a killing. That is why I never put too much pressure on the knife when I stabbed him in the back,' I answered.

'Why did you not call the police when you knew you had a dead man in the house?' asked Wilkins.

'Well I was worried about being treated the same as the Norfolk farmer who was recently jailed for life,' I replied.

'Is that why you tried to hide the body?' pressed Wilkins.

'Well, yes,' I replied nervously, thinking that my chances of escaping a heavy punishment were not going at all well.

'One final question. Why did you move the body from a farmer's field Guildford to a wooded area in Southampton?' requested Wilkins.

'For the same reason I buried him in the first place. I didn't want to be found out. There was an investigation going on in that area for a murder which was totally unrelated,' I replied.

'No further questions,' said Wilkins 'I would like to call my witness which is Doctor Phelps.'

An elderly man with grey hair and thick dark black eyebrows took the stand and was sworn in.

'Would you please state your full name and your profession,'

'My name is Donald Walker Phelps and I am the Doctor who acted as coroner for the family of the deceased.'

'Did you examine the body after it had been exhumed?' asked Wilkins.

'Yes I did,' agreed Phelps.

'Could you please explain the main relevant parts restricted to the cause of death written in your report,' requested Wilkins.

'Yes,' said Phelps, 'the body was partly decomposed, so I was able to check physical signs in the bone structure and damage to part of the internal organs. There were cut marks high on the thorax at the back of the victim between two of the ribs as if damaged by a sharp instrument. There were also cut marks on the lower ribs to the front of the body, also damaged by a sharp instrument.'

I was shocked at what I had just heard and leaned towards Cleaver and whispered in his ear.

'Mr. Cleaver, I never stabbed Brown in the front of the body, I was standing behind him.'

'Are you sure?' Cleaver returned in a whisper.

'Definitely,' I answered.

'On what you found could the damage you have mentioned been caused by a knife?' asked Wilkins.

'Yes, it could have easily have been a sharp blade,' agreed Phelps.

'Would that have caused the victim's death?' asked Wilkins.

'Yes, it would because the aorta artery was punctured. The flow of blood from the heart that would normally be pumped around the body was escaping through this damaged artery,' replied Phelps.

'No further questions,' said Wilkins.

Cleaver then rose to his feet.

'Doctor Phelps, in your opinion what stab wound would have caused the victim's death. The one in the front of the body or the one in the back?' asked Cleaver.

'The knife wound in the back of the body did not pierce the deceased's body too deeply and may, at worst, would have only punctured a lung. This would not have been enough to be fatal within the time that Brown died. Whereas the knife wound in the front was deep, puncturing the main artery and would have without doubt caused the death of Brown,' insisted Phelps.

'In addition,' added Phelps, 'my autopsy is backed up by the position the body was laying in the carpet.'

'The carpet?' queried Cleaver.

'Yes,' continued Phelps, 'the body was rolled up in an unusually patterned carpet. There was a large image of a diamond inlaid into the carpet which was distinctly soaked in blood, this part of the carpet was against the chest of the victim.'

'But wouldn't blood have soaked into the carpet at the time of the stabbing?' asked Cleaver.

'Yes, but because the victim was rolled into the carpet, the effusion of blood to the area I have described would have been at its heaviest,' explained Phelps.

'My client says he made a single stab wound to the victim's back,' said Cleaver, 'so how do you explain another stab wound to the front of the chest?'

'It is not up to me to speculate what happened, only to determine the cause of death,' answered Phelps.

'Thank you, no further questions,' said Cleaver and sat down.

At this moment the court was adjourned until the following day.

Cleaver took the opportunity to see me in my cell after the court had closed.

'Look you must tell me the truth,' he said, 'did you stab Brown in the front of the chest?'

'No I can confirm categorically that I did not,' I persisted.

'Then how do you explain the knife wound found by Phelps?' asked Cleaver.

'I only wish I knew. Could Phelps have been mistaken?' I asked.

'I doubt it, this man is a top physician and if he was not certain, his professional integrity would be at stake,' remarked Cleaver. 'In fact I would rather trust him than believe you at this point.'

Cleaver's answer was a big shock to me as it now appeared that the lawyer I had selected to defend me was having grave doubts on the information I had given him.

'Unless Joy did it. After all she was the only other person in the room,' I said.

'What? You seem to be blaming your wife now, when you were holding the knife all the time,' remarked Cleaver.

'Well, I was completely shocked to learn about the knife wound in the front of the chest although at the time I did notice a lot of blood coming from his chest. Joy may have had a knife of her own. I did see a knife lying on the floor in the corner of the room. Also, she had a lot more blood on her than I did,' I told Cleaver.

'If what you are speculating proves to be right, then that puts a completely different aspect on the case. We will have to try and find your wife,' said Cleaver, 'give me her last known address and we will follow it up. I will let you know how we get on tomorrow morning before we go into court.'

Cleaver left me to my thoughts and a very long night. The next morning I waited anxiously in anticipation of the news Cleaver would bring me. When Cleaver did eventually turn up the news was not good.

'I'm sorry,' said Cleaver, 'we did our best at trying to track down your wife, but unfortunately she has moved from the address you gave me to an unknown location.

Cleaver's news was a terrible blow for me as my only hope of a rescue was fast disappearing. All I could do now was to rely on Cleaver's skill in court.

By afternoon the same day, the court had reassembled. Looking round the court I noticed the presence of Peter Brown and his wife, the parents of Ralph. I pretended not to see them, even though they were staring in my direction.

It was time to listen to the summing up by both the prosecution and the defence.

Wilkins for the prosecution rose to his feet first and faced the jury and gave his address.

'The defendant is a man who acts before he thinks. I can cite my claim in many ways. Firstly he stabs an intruder who entered his house in the back and chest, then he tries to cover his crime by hiding the body in a farmer's field, then he moves the body when he realises that his crime may be discovered and digs a new grave just outside Southampton. These actions are clearly that of a guilty man who took the law into his own hands and at all times ignored involvement with the legal authorities. The intruder, Ralph Brown didn't posses a weapon and Wallace and his wife did not sustain any injuries during their ordeal. I put it to you that this was a deliberate murder and suggest the only verdict you as jurors can give is guilty.'

Wilkins resumed his seat appearing rather pleased with his delivery. I had to admit that he had succinctly given a good description of what had happened and his clever portrayal of events didn't give me any confidence of a successful outcome for me at this trial.

Cleaver then rose to his feet to give his summary.

'On the night in question, Richard Wallace and his wife were left in terror as they heard someone moving about their house while they lay in their bed. Extreme fear drove the defendant to arm himself with a weapon. At the time he did this, he was not aware that the intruder was unarmed. When he entered the lounge he was horrified by what he saw, which was Ralph Brown's hands clasped firmly around the neck of his wife Joy in a strangle hold, immediately perceiving her to be in grave danger. A physical attempt in trying to remove Brown from his wife didn't work. Fearing for his wife, a moment of adrenalin had set in and he instinctively directed the knife into the back of Brown hoping this would be sufficient for the intruder to release his grip on Joy's throat. However we now discover from scientific evidence that the wound to the back was not deep enough to cause death. My client says that although he accepts causing the wound to Brown's back, he did not plunge the knife in the chest to the front of the body, inferring that a third person may have been involved. With so much doubt surrounding this case the jury's only course of action is to return a verdict of not guilty.'

The judge requested the jury to retire to come up with a verdict.

After four long hours everyone was summoned to return to court.

The judge asked the foreman if the jury had arrived at a verdict.

'Yes', said the foreman, 'we have a unanimous decision and find the defendant guilty as charged.'

The judge turned his attention to the sentencing.

'Mr Wallace,' the judge said, 'you stabbed an unarmed man in the back, and then stabbed him in the chest thereby causing his death and for that I have no alternative than to pass a life sentence of confinement with a recommendation that you will not be released until you have served at least twenty five years. Take him down.'

I couldn't believe what I was hearing and found my legs wobbling after the judge's harsh words. It was like he was talking to a hardened criminal and I was nothing of the sort. The words had hardly left the judges lips when two police officers frogmarched me out of the court to a waiting van.

I was then driven to a category A prison just outside Manchester. I was strip searched and subjected embarrassingly to intense scrutiny in every orifice of my body. Then I was made to shower and given the standard prison clothing to put on. Extreme fear came over me as I braced myself for a long haul of confinement.

Chapter 10 Prison

Prison had been sampled by me before, but that was nothing compared with the establishment to which I had been taken. The building housed some of the meanest looking people I had ever seen.

From my last experience in prison I could see by comparison that it was like a kindergarten when matched against my current new surroundings. The prison housed a collection of heavy muscle bound men, many of whom would kill their own grandmother if circumstances dictated a mere minor feeling of discontent. How I was going to endure at least twenty five years of this living hell was something I wasn't keen to dwell on for any length of time.

After a quick introduction to a prison officer I was led into a small cell which I had to share with a man called Roy. My new cell mate was small and slim with mousy brown hair and was totally at odds in manner and appearance when compared with the other inmates in the establishment. He appeared a very nervous person and occasionally stuttered. I was surprised and thankful to receive a friendly greeting from him when I was introduced.

After the preliminary discussions about ourselves, we chatted away as if we had known each other years and thankful that Roy had been chosen as my room mate.

'What are you in here for?' I asked.

'Murder, the same as you,' he replied,

I looked him up and down weighing up the stature of the man.

'Surely someone has made a mistake, you didn't really kill anyone, did you? I asked.

'There has been no mistake, I killed my wife for having an affair with another man,' Roy replied.

'Really,' I remarked, 'you don't look the type to kill anyone.'

'Well, it was unfortunate, I acted on impulse, had I committed the same crime in France I wouldn't be facing a life sentence now. They would have called it a crime of passion which meets certain criteria of concessions,' he explained.

'Anyway, I can say the same about you. You don't look like the sort of person that would kill anyone or even resort to violence,' he observed.

'Even though I have been charged with murder, I don't believe I am a cold blooded killer or even a violent thug, but here I am doing time for it,' I replied.

'What is it like in here?' I asked.

'Oh it's purgatory, after all this is a category 'A' prison. I hate every minute of it. There is a lot of bullying going on in here amongst the inmates. Three, I can name, Luke, Pete and Jason. Keep clear of those I have mentioned. They are all bad as one another. These guys are bone breakers. There seems to be some sort of power struggle between the three of them and it's best to keep out of it,' related Roy.

I couldn't help noticing that Roy seemed quite eloquent in his use of the English language and generally well educated.

'Did you have a job before you came into prison?' I enquired.

'Yes, I was an Architect. In fact I had my own business. It all had to close down when I came in here,' related Roy.

The cell doors were opened and Roy indicated to me that it was time for lunch. I made sure I kept close to Roy, following his every move, although I could see by his physical appearance and nervous disposition, he would be no good as a protector if the occasion had arisen whereby I was subjected to physical assault by another inmate. However I was keen not to step out of the adopted methods of procedure, so Roy was to be my mentor until I had a better understanding of the established rules, not just those made by the authorities but also those set by the hardened criminals in the confinement. On entering the dining hall I quickly glanced around. This was the first time I had seen some of the other prisoners, a bigger collection of mean looking felons I had never before witnessed under one roof.

I lined up with the others while I was dished out with various portions of meat and vegetables and then found a seat next to Roy. Ever mindful of the new distressing surroundings that I was forced to endure, my thoughts were also dominated by inequitable feelings that I shouldn't have been incarcerated and wondered if things would have been any different if Cleaver had found Joy.

A large bald headed heavily tattooed man sat opposite me and immediately dug his fork into some of the contents on my plate, messily transferring them onto his own. I started to rise to my feet in objection, but was immediately dragged back down to my seat by Roy.

'That's Pete,' whispered Roy, 'let him take what he wants and don't get involved.'

Pete heard what Roy had said to me, because he answered in agreement.

'He's right you know if you wonna stay elthy,' answered Pete.

This was my first experience of the bully boy tactics. In the exercise yard, fights were a common occurrence. I noticed also that sometimes the prison officials would turn a blind eye if arguments among the more dominant inmates became physical. My initial introduction into this part of the prison, witnessed a physical altercation between Luke and Jason, two of the men that Roy mentioned whom I should avoid. These two were really big men which could exert extreme physical damage on each other. From the amount of blood flowing, that is exactly what was happening.

'Come on,' said Roy, 'it doesn't do to hang around when trouble is brewing.' He dragged me away and we moved to a different part of the yard.

Every day was like walking on eggshells, plus you needed eyes in the back of your head. I was constantly looking to see who was behind me and became very nervous if it was one of the big three.

Two years past by and in that time I had suffered a broken nose and one broken arm and received a large scar on the face, as a result of a problem with Luke. After the violence imposed by this man, I knew that if I was to escape future damage to my person, I had to become friendly with at least one of the trio of the heavy brigade. Although there was not much to choose between Pete, Luke and Jason, on considerable study of their behavioural patterns I noticed that Jason was probably the more approachable than the other two. With considerable effort, which involved, grovelling and acting as Jason's personal servant and slave, I managed to win Jason over. This practically guaranteed my safety against other inmates in the prison who were bent on unprovoked attacks and violence.

The very sight of Jason would scare anyone. He had a shaven head, tattoos over most of his body, including his face and weighed approximately twenty six stone. In a rare conversation I had with Jason, I was able to learn quite a lot about him. It was no surprise that he was doing time for grievous bodily harm, but he did seem to know a lot of shady characters on the outside. One day I was talking with him over lunch.

'I understand you keep in constant contact with your friends outside the prison,' I commented to Jason.

'That's right Rick, there are nastier people on the outside than there are in ere, but they are the clever ones because they never get caught,' said Jason.

'Why is it necessary to keep in close contact with these people? I asked.

'Listen Rick, if ever you are released from prison and you need some help to control someone that has upset yer, I can arrange it so that they will never do it again,' advised Jason.

'That's very good of you Jason, but I think I would prefer to stay on the right side of the law, because if I was lucky enough to be released by the establishment, I wouldn't want to return to this style of living,' I replied. I pondered over Jason's suggestion and quickly became aware that not only would the poor unfortunate victim never repeat the error they had made, they would probably never walk again.

'Well, think about what I told yer, you never know when you will need some help,' said Jason.

'That's very kind of you, it's something I'll always remember,' I answered.

*

It was a hot summer's day when I was surprised to receive a visit from Alice. It had been almost two years since I last saw Alice and had no reason to think that I would ever see her again.

In the visiting room I saw Alice sitting behind one of the glass booths and walked over to greet her.

'How are you?' I asked. 'This is a pleasant surprise. You really do look great.'

I looked Alice up and down and noticed by the clothes she was wearing she had gone to a lot of trouble for her prison visit. She was wearing a white blouse with a light grey top and matching skirt.

'Oh, I'm okay, I'm married now,' she revealed.

I found myself dismayed by this remark, and therefore had to ask the question.

'Well in that case Alice, why are you visiting me?'

'There has been some good news turned up on the horizon and I thought it was essential that I seek you out and tell you about it,' said Alice.

'I could do with some good news, things have not been exactly too cheery in here,' I admitted.

'I've really come to see you in a professional capacity,' Alice revealed.

'Well I have to tell you that I have another twenty three years to go,' I confirmed.

Alice ignored my comment and wasted no time in telling me her main reason for her visit.

'I have just read in the newspaper about the 'Norfolk farmer who killed a teenage intruder entering his property,' said Alice. 'In many respects the case was similar to yours.'

'Yes I know, I'm familiar with the case. He got life the same as me,' I said.

'The only difference is that he has now been released on appeal,' Alice pointed out. 'Not only that, news of his release has won the approbation of the media.'

'Well that is good news,' I said. 'Are you suggesting there is hope for me?'

'Indeed I am, because we can use the Norfolk farmer's release as a test case, and with your permission Rick, I will apply to the court of appeal and set the wheels in motion, hopefully I can try and get your release,' suggested Alice.

'Please do,' I agreed, believing that there was a slim chance that I could escape the agony of my dreadful current living standards, 'the sooner the better,' I added.

'Look Rick, I can not promise miracles on the outcome, but I will do my best to bring this back to the attention of the legal system as soon as humanly possible,' confirmed Alice.

'Oh, that's wonderful news,' I said with glee.

'However, I must warn you to be patient, because these things do not happen overnight and from my experience it could take a long time. Also don't raise your hopes too high, because we may not even get our day in court,' said Alice.

The visitor's bell went so it was time for Alice to leave. As I watched her go through the door I was left with a little bit of hope, which with good fortune could turn into reality. I was also left with the disappointment in the knowledge of Alice having found a new soul mate to spend the rest of her life with.

When I saw Roy I related my good news to him which was not exactly met with ecstasy.

'I know I should be happy for you, but I am not,' said Roy despondently, 'if you do manage to leave here, then I would have lost a dear friend and you need friends in here.'

I could see his point, but I couldn't let Roy's views worry me. Getting out of this living hell was the only thing on my mind. The next few days appeared longer than normal as I yearned to hear some news from Alice. Just as I had given up hope, I received a visit from her.

'Yes,' she said, 'success, the Court of appeal has been arranged for the 4th August,' Alice informed with a smile.

'That's only three weeks away,' I confirmed.

'Yes, I was thinking of asking Cleaver to put forward our case for the appeal as he does know the file quite well,' suggested Alice.

'I don't mind who you use, so long as you get me out of here,' I replied.

The day of my appeal had arrived and I found myself with mixed feelings, for although I had looked forward to my time in court I was apprehensive about the outcome.

During the case I was asked the same questions I had answered so often before and had to endure the same experiences that I had tried so desperately to extinguish from my mind.

I waited nervously while Cleaver put forward an excellent case on my behalf, citing the Norfolk farmer's appeal as a test case. His final summing up detailed the similarities between the two cases indicating the same disastrous results. Alice was right in her choice of Cleaver, because it would have been a very dispassionate judge not to grant a release having heard the eloquent oratory delivered by my learned lawyer.

The judge did however have issues regarding my part in the illegal disposal of Brown's body, but felt that I had already paid the price in the two year term that I had served.

As a result I was granted an immediate release from prison.

Although I was delighted by this news I was unable to stop media release of the result of the appeal, which put my photograph well and truly on the front page of all the national newspapers.

Having been released from prison, I now had to find somewhere to stay. My immediate thoughts were to return to Bournemouth and the Guest House owned by Janice. It was a complete revelation not to be hounded by the police and satisfyingly knowing that I could go anywhere in the country without hiding or worrying about being recognised. In fact I found the opposite to be the case, because those that did recognise me treated me like some kind of celebrity.

When I arrived at the Guest House, Janice greeted me with a big hug and fussed over me like a mother hen. I wasn't sure that I could cope with this extreme adulation, as it was something I had never been accustomed. We sat down in the lounge and had an endless chat. We talked about my time in prison and Janice was keen to know what I was going to do next.

'Janice, I know I have been released from prison by a judge, but in the eyes of the public I have not been completely vindicated, because they still believe that I killed Ralph Brown.' I said.

'Well you did, didn't you?' replied Janice.

'At the time of that fateful night I really thought that I had killed him, but now after the court case, a seed of doubt has been planted in my mind,' I said.

'A seed of doubt?' queried Janice.

'Yes the coroner's evidence after his autopsy indicated a stab wound in the front of the chest and I know that the weapon I held made no contact with that part of his body,' I confirmed.

'What are you going to do now?' Janice asked.

'I must find Joy, because she was the only other person in the room,' I said. 'I will therefore hole up here for a few days and then I will see if I can find her.'

'Well I wish you well on that one, but don't be too disappointed if you don't get the result you are seeking,' replied Janice.

The following day I woke to bright flashing lights which appeared to be coming from outside. I drew open the curtains only to find that the flashing lights were from the cameras of the paparazzi. My release from prison had obviously generated national awareness which I had no interest in perpetuating, so I closed the curtains and never ventured outside the Guest House. I concluded that I must have been followed after my release.

Two days later Janice knocked on my door.

'There is a man here to see you downstairs,' said Janice.

'If he is from the newspapers, I don't want to know,' I replied.

'He says, he is not from the newspapers, but claims he knows you,' said Janice.

I rushed down the stairs to the front door to see who my mystery visitor was, only to be confronted with Peter Brown, Ralph's father. I was dumbstruck at seeing him and waited for him to speak first.

'Hello Rick, I thought I would find you here. Aren't you going to invite me in?' asked Peter.

'Yes, of course,' I replied. I showed Peter into the lounge not knowing why he had come to see me or what to expect.

'How did you know I was here?' I asked.

'Well it wasn't difficult, you have been in all the newspapers, also this Guest House in which you have been staying has had a lot of press coverage,' Peter replied.

'Now you have gone to a lot of trouble and have found me, I assume that it is not to offer me a job or enquire about my health,' I said.

'Definitely not,' Peter replied, 'I have come here to give you the same treatment you gave my son.'

Not expecting this remark from Peter I started to back away. Then I saw the glint of steel in his hand, which I assumed to be a knife slightly masked by a fold in the side of his jacket. I started to back away further, whereupon Peter lunged at me with the weapon. The knife managed to make contact with my arm. In seconds my shirt sleeve was soaked in blood and I felt a sharp pain running through my body.

'Don't do anything stupid,' I begged Peter holding up my hand in front of me.

I managed to dodge another lunge by Peter, but fell off balance in the process and dropped to the floor. Peter then took advantage of the precarious position catching me in the side of the chest. In that moment Janice walked into the lounge to witness the whole drama of what was happening before her eyes. She let out a scream and Peter turned brushed passed her and ran out of the house still carrying the knife.

'Quick, get me an ambulance,' I called to Janice at the same time trying unsuccessfully to stop blood dripping onto her carpet. She immediately did what I asked and within minutes a paramedic was dealing with my wounds.

'You're lucky,' said the paramedic, 'the knife just glanced the side of your chest, so it really appears worse than it actually is.'

At the hospital my wounds received attention and I was able to return to the Guest House the same day.

'You really ought to inform the police about this incident,' urged Janice.

'No!' I said emphatically, 'I can understand his behaviour in a way, and I would hate this to get into the newspapers. I only hope that if he discovers that he has not done any lasting damage then he will not return to complete what he intended to do.'

In the days that followed Janice was the perfect carer in nursing me back to health. I wasn't sure why she had stood by me in all the time that I knew her, because since I had arrived at the Guest House all I had been was trouble to her with a capital 'T'.

Chapter 11 Looking for Joy

I knew that in order to vindicate myself of the crime to which I had been accused and gain a bit of self respect; I had to find Joy. I began by calling on her last known address which was her sister's house, even though I had been informed by Cleaver that she no longer lived there. I wasn't sure how I was going to be received, so I knocked gingerly on the door. Sylvia answered the door, smiled, gave me a big hug and invited me in. I was surprised by her reaction at seeing me, but pleased nevertheless, because it appeared that she held no animosity against me.

'Rick. What brings you here?' asked Sylvia with her usual friendly smile.

Sylvia being a twin sister to Joy was almost identical in appearance to Joy, although in attitude she had a more fun aspect to life. It was difficult sometimes to tell them apart and when they were together I often muddled them up.

'Sylvia, I'm trying to find Joy, and this I believe was her last known address,' I replied.

'Well she did stay here for a while after she separated from you Rick, but she has since left here and I have no idea where she is at the moment. In fact another man was looking for her earlier and I had to tell him the same thing,' explained Sylvia.

'What happened Sylvia? Why did she leave?' I asked.

'Well, we did have a bit of a falling out and she left. I have since tried to get hold of her on her mobile phone, but she has appeared to have had it changed. I really don't think she wants to be found,' explained Sylvia.

'If you do hear from her, you will inform me won't you, as it is important that I speak to her?' I requested.

'Certainly, but I don't expect I will ever hear from her again,' replied Sylvia.

I left Sylvia's house feeling disappointed and none the wiser about Joy's whereabouts, not having the first clue where to begin my searching.

My first thoughts were to speak to Alice to see if she had any ideas about finding a lost person. Although she would not know where Joy could be located, at least she could probably provide some good advice to put me on the right track. When I called at Alice's house she had just come back from doing some shopping as I met her at the garden gate.

'What are you doing here?' asked Alice in surprise.

'Well, I was hoping you can give me some advice,' I replied.

'I'll try, but I can't promise anything,' said Alice, 'come on in and I'll see if I can help.'

Alice led the way into the house and I followed.

'Alice, if you were looking for someone and they had recently moved but you did not know their new address, where would you begin your first investigations?' I asked.

'Ooh that's a difficult one,' replied Alice, 'I'm not sure you are asking the right person here.'

'Look Alice I don't even know where to start looking and I am desperate to find this person,' I replied.

'Firstly who are you trying to find?' enquired Alice.

'Joy, I need some important information from her,' I answered.

'It's a long shot, but firstly I would contact her mother and if that didn't work I would speak to her friends,' Alice advised.

'Of course, her mother, that's a good start,' I concurred, 'I hadn't thought of her.'

'One more question for you,' I said, 'the new man that you are with, are you happy with him?' I asked.

'Yes I am, surely you didn't think there was any chance for the two of us,' replied Alice.

'Well, I was hoping,' I said.

'Look Rick, a little while ago you were facing a jail term of life imprisonment. I couldn't wait a period of at least twenty five years for you to return to normal civilisation and that is why I didn't visit you in jail. If I had known that you were going to be released early, things may have been different between us,' stated Alice.

Although I found Alice's answer really depressing, I could understand that she needed to get on with her life. Waiting around for me to be released after a possible twenty five years would not have allowed her to do this.

I thanked Alice for her assistance and drove off, my thoughts in turmoil as I drove back to the Guest House, regarding the changed circumstances that had evolved between my one time lover and myself.

The following day I headed off towards Joy's mother Doris, who I had always had a close affinity with in the past. I hoped the breakup between Joy and me would not affect our previous close relationship. There was only one way to find out. I knocked apprehensively on the door. Doris opened the door and the broad smile that came over her face, told me that she held no feelings of animosity against me and immediately put me at my ease.

'Rick,' she said, 'it's really you. Come on in.' Doris who was a grey haired lady with blue eyes and small in stature invited me into the lounge.

'Doris,' I said, 'I'm trying to find the whereabouts of Joy.'

'Are you Rick, but does Joy wish to be found?' said Doris posing the question to herself.

'Do you know where she can be found?' I asked in earnest.

'Yes, I do know her current address, but I am unable to give it to you, because Joy has asked me not to divulge this to anyone, especially you Rick.'

'Do you know if she is working?' I asked.

'Yes, she is working in York at a carpet factory, the same place where your carpet came from. You know the one with the blue diamond on it. That is all the information I am going to give you and I repeat I will never give you her address,' advised Doris.

I thanked Doris, and left. Doris without realising it had provided me with a window of opportunity, but I still had to do a bit more probing, which involved a lot of asking of questions.

Recalling the carpet fitter who supplied our flamboyant floor covering was not coming immediately to my mind.

It was then that I had wished I had paid more attention when Joy told me the name of the supplier. However there were three carpet fitters in the town, so I knew it wouldn't take long to go round to all of them.

The first two shops I tried couldn't help me at all. One of the shops was bought by a new owner, which meant that the details of any purchases of two years ago would be lost. I was almost at the point of giving up when I ventured into the last shop which was Donald Jones, Carpet fitters.

'Donald, do you remember a bespoke carpet being fitted by your company at my old address, the colour was red inlaid with a distinctive fluorescent blue diamond? Was it your shop that supplied it?' I enquired.

'Remember it, how could I forget it. I have never seen a carpet like it before in my life and I don't suppose I will ever see one like it again,' replied Donald.

'Good,' I sighed, 'can you give me the address of the manufacturer?'

'That may be difficult, you see we deal with several manufacturers,' replied Donald.

'Oh, I think I can narrow that down for you, because I believe it came from York,' I said.

'Right, just a minute, I'll look it up. Yes, it came from Tenants Carpets, of 1b River Industrial Estate, York.

Why do you ask? Do you want another one?' asked Donald.

'No thank you, but thank you very much for your information,' I replied and quickly vacated the shop, leaving behind me a very puzzled shop keeper.

My next task was to take the long journey to York and find the address given to me by Donald Jones. Throughout the journey I was hoping that my drive would not prove to be a wasted effort on my part. When I arrived in York it was evening, so I immediately booked into a hotel. I intended to complete my detective work early in the morning when I knew that there was a possibility Joy would be at work.

The next morning I was up early and ready to find Tenants Carpets and Joy.

It was not difficult finding the industrial estate or the carpet manufacturer and everything appeared to be going to plan. I asked the Secretary in the office if I could speak to Mrs Wallace and sat in the waiting room rehearsing the questions I was going to ask Joy. While I was waiting I was looking around the room and my eyes were drawn to a picture on the wall. It was a photograph of the very same diamond pattern that at one time graced our lounge. It seemed that wherever I went something would be said or I would be confronted with an image which would remind me of the worst day in my life on that June evening.

It wasn't long before Joy appeared in the waiting room flushed and ready to tear into me.

'What are you doing here?' she asked shocked at seeing her surprise visitor.

'Look Joy I have to speak to you about something of extreme importance and it is something that can't wait,' I urged.

'Not here, I'm at work and I am very busy,' she whispered as she edged me nearer the door.

'Where and when can I see you then?' I asked not wishing to be put off.

'Meet me at the house I am currently renting out, at six o'clock this evening,' said Joy who quickly scribbled an address on a scrap of paper and handed it to me.

'Alright, but if this proves to be a false address, then I will return here in the morning,' I commented.

Joy did not answer me and disappeared through the waiting room door.

Promptly at six o'clock I was at the address Joy had given me. Joy greeted me with a look of despair and invited me in the house.

'Well I wish I could say that it is nice to see you, but it wouldn't be true,' said Joy.

'This is not a social call, so I 'm not expecting any pleasantries between us,' I replied.

'Then why are you here?' asked Joy, 'and please get to the point quickly.'

'I want to talk to you about that fateful day in June approximately two years ago, when Ralph Brown entered our house,' I said.

Joy heaved a big sigh as if it was a subject she no longer wanted to discuss.

'Do you mean the day you stabbed an unarmed man and did time for it,' remarked Joy.

I noticed Joy was immediately on the offensive and didn't waste an opportunity in reminding me of the crime to which I had been convicted.

'Yes, I mean exactly that day,' I confirmed, although not happy about Joy's sarcasm about the related incident or the manner of her obvious confrontation.

'In fact, I'm surprised they let you out,' Joy added smiling at my obvious discomfort.

I tried to ignore the fact that she was trying to goad me into an argument and tried to steer her with a more friendly approach.

'Listen to me Joy, the forensic evidence pointed to the fact that Ralph Brown was stabbed in the front of the chest. Now, I know that I made only one stab wound and that was to his back. I couldn't have attacked him in the front, because I was behind him.'

Joy remained silent and started looking up at the ceiling and then around the walls, in fact anywhere but directing her gaze to me. I knew from her attitude that I had mentioned something that she didn't want to talk about, but also something I needed to pursue until I got some definitive answers.

'Did you have a weapon on you at the time you were in the lounge?' I asked.

'I may have done and there again I may not have,' said Joy being evasive and looking away.

'Look Joy, this is not some kind of game. I must know if you armed yourself before you walked into the lounge,' I urged.

'Well of course I did, I picked up a knife from the bedroom drawer. I wasn't going to go into any of the ground floor rooms unarmed knowing there was an intruder in the house. In fact you were exactly the same. You also carried a dangerous weapon,' admitted Joy.

'Yes I am aware of that,' I concurred, 'but, tell me did you use the weapon you were carrying on him? I asked.

'When he put a strangle hold on me, I had to do something, so yes, like you, I did use the knife,' replied Joy.

'Do you mean to say that you let me take the rap for this? After all the trouble I was suffering, you never came forward when I was arrested,' I argued.

'Well there was no point in both of us going to jail, you also had a hand in killing him,' said Joy.

It was at this point of our discussions, I realised I had made an error in not bringing with me a small battery operated Dictaphone to record the incriminating words that Joy was relating about the incident.

'Apparently the forensic evidence indicates that my actions did not constitute towards Ralph's death, but the stab wound executed to the chest was in fact the fatal blow. That action was taken and caused by you Joy and you alone.'

'Well it's all academic now. You have already done some time for it and the police are not looking for anyone else, so I can't see what advantage it would be dragging the whole thing through the courts again,' said Joy in a matter of fact manner.

I found it difficult to comprehend Joy's phlegmatic attitude. The mere fact that she wished to distance herself from the whole episode angered me enormously.

'Listen Joy, in the eyes of the public I am still a guilty man. I have already had Peter Brown attacking me with a knife in which I was lucky to escape with my life,' I explained.

'I think you ought to go to the police and admit everything you have told me,' I suggested.

'I'm not admitting to anything,' argued Joy 'and if you go to the police I shall deny everything. In fact it will be your word against mine and remember you have already been convicted of the crime.'

'Look Joy. The law has changed. If you tell them that you stabbed Brown in self defence, you will probably get away with it,' I pointed out.

'No!' Joy said stubbornly, 'I am not going to take that chance.'

'Looking back, it has been me that has done all the worrying, hiding from the police, facing court actions and finally done a spell in prison. You on the other hand have had a trouble free existence,' I pointed out.

'You always were a bit of a wimp,' ranted Joy. 'Anyway, I'm glad you managed to contact me, because I need your current address, as I intend to file for a divorce.'

I complied with her request with full satisfaction by writing the address of the Guest House down on a piece of paper and handed it to her. I was as anxious to split the marriage partnership permanently as she was.

'Now if you don't mind Rick, I don't think we have anything further to talk about, so I shall ask you to leave,' Joy urged.

'You haven't heard the last of this Joy, if you won't make a confession to the police, then I will get you to make one through the courts,' I insisted as I began to leave.

On the drive back home I was seething at Joy's attitude of apathy and general feeling of apparent lack of interest. Also her revelation of taking advantage of my visit to advance the divorce, added to my anger.

When I arrived back at the Guest House I related the whole experience of my discussions I had with Joy to Janice who was most supportive, sympathetic and understanding to my plight.

'Rick having made the threat of court action to Joy, you must pursue it,' said Janice.

I thought about Janice's comment and wondered whether it would be worth the aggravation of returning to court.

Chapter 12 Good Fortune

I tried to put the whole York day experience out of my mind. My finances from the share of the sale of the house was dwindling fast, having expended most of it on day to day living and paying accommodation fees to Janice. I had to find myself a job and find one quickly. The problem in finding work was that there were not many building sites in the area and those that were active had either passed the stage of bricklaying or had all the labour that they needed. My desperation was such that I contemplated trying to find work further away but in order to do this I would have had to vacate the Guest House and Janice's good cooking.

Then one day Janice tapped on my room door. At the time I was gathering all my belongings together ready to move out.

'I've got a little bit of good news for you,' said Janice. 'The lottery ticket, you left me to check, proved good on the first three numbers. You have ten pounds to collect at the local newsagent.'

'Okay, that's good, thank you for checking that for me,' I replied, 'I have to go to the bank to withdraw some money, I will collect it at the same time.'

I decided to inform Janice of my departure after I had returned from the Town.

It was raining so I wasn't enjoying my walk to the bank. Having drawn out my money and leaving a meagre balance of money remaining in my account, I began to wonder whether or not to walk the entire length of the high street in such dreadful weather to pick up my small winnings. *'Well'*, I thought, *'one day I might be glad of a tenner and I am not exactly that well off.'*

By the time I had reached the newsagent I was soaked right through to the skin. I felt ridiculous at having done the extra walk in such inclement weather for such a pitiful amount of money and contemplated whether it was worth all the trouble.

'I believe I'm due ten pounds,' I said handing the assistant the lottery ticket and at the same time picking up a magazine on vintage cars and trying to work out whether my current finances could afford it or not.

She took the ticket and placed it into the checker machine. Paused for a good few seconds and then looked up at me and then back at her machine. By this time I had decided that the magazine was a luxury I couldn't afford and placed it neatly back on the book rack.

'Is there something wrong?' I asked.

'Yes,' she said, 'I can't pay you out.'

I thought to myself, *'that's all I needed having drenched myself to get there and I really needn't have bothered.'* By this time I had worked myself up into a really bad mood and wanted to take it out on someone but didn't know who. I thought of Janice who must have made a mistake in checking the numbers.

'Why not? I asked, 'don't I have the requisite amount of correct winning numbers.'

'Oh yes,' she said, 'you have the right numbers alright, the only problem is that you have six winning numbers, and I can't pay out jackpots.'

She was so expressionless in giving her answer, that I asked her to repeat it.

I couldn't believe that I was hearing correctly and asked the assistant to say it for a third time.

'You have a line of six winning numbers. Are you deaf?' she asked emphasising the word 'deaf'.

I was so ecstatic that I ignored the insult from the assistant with the enigmatic manner.

'How much have I won?' I asked.

'Oh, something in excess of nine million pounds if you are the only one with a ticket containing these numbers, I can't be sure of the exact figure, you will have to contact the lottery organisers. Here's your ticket back, right who's next,' she answered still not changing the expression on her face.

'I want to buy this magazine,' I said retrieving it for a second time off the rack.

It was true then, I had managed somehow to conjure up some good fortune and to think that I had a moment when I wasn't going to cash the ticket in. My body started to go through every stage of physical emotion. I started shaking, feeling hot, then feeling cold and finally unable to speak. I didn't remember the walk back to the Guest House in the bad weather, I seemed to be in my own little world as if walking on air. When I entered the Guest House soaked and dripping with water, Janice was sitting in the lounge reading a newspaper.

'Did you manage to check all the numbers on the ticket,' I asked Janice.

'Well, I managed to get the first three numbers, but I was a bit slow in finding a pen and writing them down, after that the television moved to another programme and I wasn't quick enough. Did I miss a number?' asked Janice.

'Yes, you missed another three and all on the same line,' I replied. Janice looked puzzled.

'I've hit the jackpot,' I screamed, at the same time jumping up and down like a child. Such was my ecstatic behaviour. I had gone from rags to riches in the space of a momentary blink of an eye and now had the promise of a large sum of money far beyond my wildest dreams.

At that moment Janice realised the full impact of my revelation, came over to me, gave me a hug and started jumping up and down with me shouting and screaming. It was a good job no one was looking at us because they would have thought that we were asylum cases.

'Come on Janice let's open a bottle of champagne, it's not often I become a millionaire over night,' I said as I went over to Janice's glass cabinet.

We had just managed to drink our way through three quarters of the bottle, when Janice started to put a damper on my brief happiness.

'You do realise Rick, because you are not divorced you will have to give half of this money to your estranged wife, Joy.'

'She will have to find out about it first and I shan't tell her,' I replied positively.

'Oh, she will find out about it alright. It will be in all the newspapers,' said Janice.

'Of course, the newspapers. I was forgetting that they like to keep close tabs on me,' I sighed.

The following week I received the cheque from the Lottery for £9,437,442.89 together with advice from a lottery adviser on how to use the money. It was confirmed that I was the sole lottery winner and therefore rightfully entitled to the full jackpot. Janice was right, the newspapers had got hold of the story and unfortunately managed to add some other unwelcome facts regarding my spell in prison and the crime that had been committed. Joy would have been certain to have seen this snippet of news, so all I could do was wait to see what impact it would have.

I didn't have to wait long. The following day Janice announced that there was someone to see me in the lounge. I had a hunch who my visitor would be before I entered the room. Yes, I was right as I walked into the lounge I was greeted with this broad smile from Joy, who uncharacteristically hugged me as soon as I had made my appearance.

'That is a completely different greeting I received from the last time I met you,' I remarked.

'Well, yes,' she accepted, 'I have been thinking that maybe I was a bit too hasty on suggesting a divorce. I want to see if we can try again and maybe recapture the happiness we once shared. I know if we tried we could do it.'

'I'm sorry Joy, I'd rather got used to the idea of a permanent separation after you mentioned it when I was in York the other day, so if you don't initiate the documentation for a divorce, then I will have to ensure that it is processed,' I insisted.

It was at that point that Joy's attitude towards me changed.

'Okay, but I understand you have come into some good fortune in the form of a lottery win and I must remind you that we are still married and would therefore be expecting at least half of the amount that you may have already received,' Joy commented.

'So that is the real reason you are here. I thought it wasn't to check on my health. Somehow I did expect a visit from you, but I didn't expect it to be quite so quick. Whatever you will be entitled to, you will get. I will promise you that,' I replied.

'Just make sure you don't forget. I shall be waiting,' Joy insisted.

'I will ask you to leave now, because I have nothing more to say to you,' I said showing Joy the door.

Two weeks later I received a Solicitor's letter indicating details of a legal separation and setting out Joy's claims in financial terms which included fifty percent of the well publicised amount I had received.

Against my better judgement and to my complete distress, I had no alternative other than to pay the demand that was made in full.

Chapter 13 Contact with Alice

An unexpected telephone call from Alice brought about a renewed contact with her. I was greeted in her office with a hug and asked to sit down.

'Is this a professional call or are you just pleased to see me?' I asked.

'Well, it's a bit of both,' replied Alice.

'Have you ever thought of implicating your wife with regard to the death of Ralph Brown?' inquired Alice.

'I have thought about it many times over since my release from prison, but I am still uncertain what to do,' I said.

'It will clear your name if you are successful,' said Alice.

'I know, I will give it some thought, but first now that the legal separation has come through I need to push ahead with a divorce,' I answered.

'As we have been seeing each other before you were arrested, it may be more pragmatic to approach another solicitor regarding your divorce,' suggested Alice.

'Yes I will take your advice. You did indicate that there was another matter you wished to see me about,' I said.

'That's right, I was thinking that maybe we should renew our relationship,' said Alice with a smile.

'I thought you were with someone else,' I replied.

'Oh, I was, but not anymore. It didn't work out because he was seeing another woman and he has now left,' answered Alice.

'I don't suppose your suggestion has anything to do with me coming into some money?' I said sarcastically.

'Of course not. What do you think I am, some mercenary money grabbing harlot,' replied Alice.

'Harlot? Definitely not. Money grabbing? I'm not so sure,' I said, 'I think I'd rather keep things as they are for the time being. That is strictly on a professional basis.'

Although I felt that Alice was a nice girl, I did think that she did not help me when she informed the police of the confidential revelation I made to her regarding my involvement in the fate of Ralph Brown.

I noticed that since winning the money I had become very popular with the opposite sex. First Joy and then Alice. I wondered who would be next knocking on my door confessing their undying love for me.

My new found fortune was undoubtedly going to change my life and it had materialised just in time because the money accrued from my share of the sale of the house where Joy and I lived, was dwindling fast, the main expenditure being day to day living expenses.

It was therefore essential that I found a permanent address to live and decided that my first priority in making use of the money would be house hunting. After days of searching I managed to secure the sale of a large property of ostentatious quality in Bournemouth for just under two million pounds.

I said my farewells to Janice who appeared quite distressed to see me leave. As I left the Guest House Janice gave me a letter which was from a solicitor; its contents sent me weak at the knees. I noted that Peter Brown was making a claim on my personal fortune as a result of the crime committed on his son Ralph.

I wasn't sure whether such a claim would have any credence in the courts but did not want to take the chance. It was now really important for me to try and completely clear my name for the death of Ralph Brown and the only way I was successfully going to achieve this was to implicate Joy's involvement. Now in the past Joy has tried to distance herself from the incident of that fateful night, believing that if there was a crime it had now been closed by the penal time I had spent in prison. It was also Joy's view that it was pointless to re-open and regenerate a completely new court case which would implicate her.

In completely disagreeing with Joy's views regarding the Ralph Brown incident I made another visit to Alice in which I confirmed that now I had adequate finance in place, I wished to proceed with her suggestion of implicating Joy and clearing my name.

Chapter 14 The Unwelcome Visitor

In my years before the time of coming into money, I had never seen inside a house with grandiose and extravagant qualities and now I was fortunate enough to be living in one. The house boasted six bedrooms all with ensuite shower rooms, a very large kitchen tastefully fitted out with oak cupboards and granite worktops. The lounge included oak doors, a stone fireplace and sliding folding doors leading to the garden. Outside there was approximately three and a half acres of ground mainly laid to lawn with great oak and willow trees strategically placed throughout the grounds. A long drive led up to a large parking area in front of the house. Towards the side of the house was a medium sized swimming pool surrounded by six life sized statues, all of which was enclosed by a honeycombed brick wall.

Such was the metamorphosis of my life that I found it difficult to adapt to the new ostentatious but grandiose style of living. I would constantly sit in my new lounge gazing and marvelling at all the things that surrounded me and constantly look out in wonderment at the view that beheld me which was rolling hills and cornfields. How lucky I was to attain such a grand place to call my home in such a short space of time, which had all become possible from the purchase of a lottery ticket. It was as if a fairy had descended on me, asked me what I wanted, waved a magic wand on my command and made everything suddenly materialise.

The only problem with a place so large was that it needed a lot of upkeep. Still I had plenty of time to do it and with the absence of callers I benefitted by the lack of interruptions.

Then one day I heard the door bell ring for the very first time. I suspiciously looked through the window to see if it was anyone I knew, because I was not aware anyone had of my latest address. No, I didn't recognise the caller, so I thought it might be a sales person or a utility meter reader.

I answered the door to see a slim man of approximately six feet two inches in height of approximately similar age to myself with dark black hair.

'Are you Richard Wallace?' asked the caller.

'Yes, that's me,' I replied.

'You don't know me. My name is Harold Wentworth, I am Joy's boy friend,' said the caller.

'But I thought Joy was living a long way from here in York,' I said.

'Not any more she lives only two miles from here, she moved address only last month,' Wentworth confirmed.

'Well anyway, I'm pleased to meet you,' I said extending my hand ready to shake his. I was quick to notice with surprise that he did not reciprocate my offer of a handshake so I withdrew my hand.

'If you have come to see me about obtaining my approval to see my wife, I can tell you now that I have no objection,' I confirmed and went to close the door. Wentworth was quick to notice and placed his right foot on the threshold to prevent a complete closure.

'No, I have come to ask you to drop the court case against Joy, it's having a terrible effect on her' said Harold forcibly.

'No, I'm afraid I can not do that,' I replied.

'Can not, or will not drop the court case?' he asked.

'Both,' I answered emphatically.

As soon as I gave my answer I noticed his eyes widen in disbelief.

'Listen to me, if you don't drop this action and drop it quickly, then I will return to persuade you in other ways and next time I will not be quite so friendly,' urged Harold.

'Friendly? I queried, 'I haven't noticed you being at all friendly. In fact you have approached me with a deliberate offensive attitude.'

'Well, that is how I like to get my point over,' he replied.

'Are you threatening me?' I asked.

'Let me say that for the moment I'm asking you to think again. You have heard what I have said and I see no need to repeat it,' replied Harold.

'Okay I will think it over,' I said, 'but can you give me your current address so that I can contact you with my answer.'

Harold stupidly, but obligingly wrote the address on a slip of paper, handed it to me and left.

This was not a visitor I wanted to see or make contact in the future and confess that in not knowing his intentions I was left in a quandary of what to do next. It was pointless phoning the police, because Harold would deny that such a conversation took place. Then I recalled a conversation I had with Jason in the prison, who at the time did offer to help if ever I was involved in a situation which required assistance. I could not think of a better example and phoned the telephone number Jason had given me when I was in prison.

'Yes, who's that,' came the voice at the other end of the phone.

'Oh, you probably haven't heard of me before, I'm Rick Wallace, a friend of Jason's,' I said.

'How is Jason?' came the reply.

'He's okay, although I haven't seen him for a while. He asked me to ring you if I had a problem and said that you are the right person who can help me,' I confided.

'That depends on what you want doing,' came the reply.

'Well, I just want you to persuade someone for me that they are being foolish,' I said.

'Oh, persuasion is my buzz word,' he answered.

'Give me your address and I will come and see you,' he urged.

I did as I was asked and gave him my address and telephone number.

'Can I take you name? I asked.

'I will give you a name, but it is not my correct name,' he said, 'let me see, call me Zach.'

The line went suddenly dead, the phone was obviously immediately replaced by Zach.

Two days later I received my second caller of the week. Again looking through the window I noticed a heavily built bald headed man standing at the door approximately six feet in height sporting an array of tattoos down both arms. His face was heavily scarred and the man appeared to walk with a pronounced limp and carried a walking stick. It was apparent from his appearance that this man had been implicated in a few battles in the past.

I stood against the door not daring to open it until I had discovered the true identity of my caller.

'Who is it?' I said cautiously.

'Zach,' came the reply, 'you phoned me the other day.'

I opened the door, and stood open mouthed at the fierce looking appearance of my caller.

'Well, aren't yer going to invite me in?' he yelled.

'Sure do come in,' I said directing him towards the lounge.

'Nice gaff you 'ave ere,' remarked Zach. 'Now what do you want to see me about?'

'I have been threatened by someone, and Jason said you can help,' I said.

'Sure I can help, any friend of Jason's is a friend of mine,' replied Zach.

I looked at this animalistic man and was not sure that I wanted him as a friend as he suggested.

'Just give me an address to go to and you will never ere from this geaser again,' promised Zach.

'Now Zach, I don't want you to rough him up too much. I want you to promise me that,' I urged.

'Oh Rick, you are taking all the fun out of it. Can't I just maim him a little bit?' asked Zach.

'No, if I thought you were going to be violent towards this man, then I would not give you his address,' I confirmed.

'Okay, said Zach, that's all agreed, now give me the address and your telephone number,' accepted Zach.

I did as I was asked.

'Now Zach, we come to the question of payment. How much do you want for doing this work?' I queried.

'All I want is two thousand pounds and my expenses, that is the cost of travelling to and from the location. Like I said any friend of Jason's is a friend of mine. Also I want a one thousand deposit,' confirmed Zach.

I was surprised that Zach wanted money up front, but paid him the agreed amount plus a sum for his travelling outgoings. After a firm shake of hands which almost broke my fingers, he was gone.

Three days later I received a telephone call from Zach confirming that I would hear no more from Harold Wentworth. Although this was refreshing to hear, I wondered whether Zach's powers of persuasion stopped short of violence and hoped that he had kept his promise.

The same day as Zach's call, I received another call on the door. Again looking through the window, I noticed my caller was Jason.

I rushed to the door and opened it to a happy looking Jason who I quickly showed into the Lounge.

'I've been released from that hell hole they call prison,' revealed Jason.

'Oh, I'm so pleased for you,' I said smiling, 'what will you do now?'

'Well I was hoping you were going to help me there,' said Jason.

'How do you mean?' I asked.

'Well, I have no where to live and I thought you might be able to help me?' said Jason.

I was definitely not happy with Jason's suggestion as I didn't like the idea of him sharing my affluent home and delayed uncomfortably my response.

'I not sure, I wasn't looking for a lodger,' I nervously replied.

'Why not? You have plenty of room ere, in fact you have enough room ere for a complete army,' insisted Jason.

With this reply I had difficulty in finding a suitable answer,, so against my better judgement, I reluctantly agreed.

Chapter 15 Problem for Joy

Jason moved in all his belongings and made himself comfortable. The only problem I found that he was a bit untidy and had obviously not been used to living on his own and looking after himself.

As time went by, making the decision to have Jason as a lodger proved to be not so bad after all. We often had long conversations and had many stories to share. When I related to him my experiences which led me to a term in prison, he seemed very interested in the circumstances surrounding the double movement of Ralph's body.

'Did yer fink you were following in the footsteps of Burke and Hare, the body snatchers in the nineteenth century?' he joked and giggled his way through the question.

'It was no laughing matter,' I said annoyed that Jason could find anything comparable with these villains or any remote form of amusement connected to my plight. 'anyway the Burke and Hare duo were making money for medical experimentation, which was clearly not something I was doing,' I continued.

Jason was still blatantly amused by what I had told him, but I was keen to get off of this unpalatable subject, so I moved onto another topic I wished to discuss with him.

'I had to call on the services of your friend Zach,' I informed him, when Jason had got over the giggles.

'Zach, I don't know any geaser called Zach,' he replied.

'That's odd,' I said.

'Was he a heavily built man like me with plenty of tattoos and walked with a limp?' Jason enquired.

'Yes, that's him,' I confirmed.

'Oh, I know who you mean. He never uses his real name, always a pseudonym as a security measure. In fact I have known im twenty years and I don't even know his real name,' replied Jason.

'Was he able to elp?' continued Jason.

'Well let's put it this way, I haven't heard anymore from the person who threatened me,' I said.

'No, and you won't,' confirmed Jason.

The door bell rang, and as it is my normal practice to rush to the window to see the identity of my visitor, on this occasion I never did, believing that I had my own resident body guard in Jason, who I could call on in times of difficulty. I opened the door to find Joy in floods of tears. Although the two of us were estranged partners, it was nevertheless upsetting to see Joy in such distress.

I beckoned Joy to come inside and took her into a room separate from the one that Jason had accommodated so that we could have some privacy.

'What has happened?' I asked.

'Well, a nasty looking thug of a man called at our door approximately a week ago and threatened Harold if he didn't leave you alone,' sobbed Joy.

'Was he violent towards him?' I enquired.

'No, but it was sufficient to make Harold leave and I don't know where he has gone,' replied Joy.

'Forgive me Joy, but I don't know why you would want to come and see me about a breakup with your boy friend. It is really of little interest to me and none of my business,' I told her.

'The trouble is that he has run off with all the money you gave me. Now I have nothing,' revealed Joy.

'What!' I exclaimed. 'How did that happen?'

'Well I opened a joint account with him and he has withdrawn every penny,' Joy stuttered.

By this time Joy had stopped crying and managed to compose herself.

'I don't suppose I can move in with you?' begged Joy, 'after all we are still married!'

'That may be true, but we are getting a divorce and I am also engineering a court action against you,' I replied, 'and I intend to go ahead with it.'

'We don't have to get divorced and you don't have to take me to court,' said Joy.

'No, I don't want you living here and yes, I am determined to clear my name for a crime I did not commit,' I confirmed.

My answer was a prelude for the tears to start rolling down her cheeks again.

'What will you do now?' I asked.

'Oh, I expect I shall go back and live with my sister, Sylvia,' sobbed Joy.

I showed Joy to the door and said my farewells. I noticed that her visit was playing on my mind a bit and wondered if I was right to have adopted a hard unwavering stance towards her. However I consoled myself that to do otherwise would mean dropping the divorce and my efforts to clear my name.

I returned to the lounge to see Jason reading the newspaper.

'Is everything alright old boy? You look a bit flushed,' remarked Jason.

'Oh, I'm okay,' I replied. At this point I thought it would be a good idea to get a second opinion from Jason about someone else on my mind, Peter Brown.

'Jason there is a man who wants to take me to court in order to get some compensation from me as a result of an earlier court case where I was committed to prison for life, although subsequently released.'

'That's a difficult one. I could go and have a word with im if yer want. I have very persuasive ways,' answered Jason.

'No, that could probably do more harm than good, and would probably go against me,' I said. I realised then that Jason was probably the wrong person to ask. It appeared that he and his unnamed friends only knew one method of solving a dispute which included violence or the threats of violence. It was time to pay my solicitor Alice a call.

My timing to see Alice could not have been better. She had just received a letter from Peter Brown's solicitor outlining the terms of his claim.

'Look Rick, I will contact Brown's solicitor and explain that there is a court case pending which will have a direct impact on the action that they wish to take. That should give us plenty of breathing time to launch our own case against your wife,' Alice advised.

Alice's advice gave me some hope and my mood was more relaxed for the journey home.

I had just made my way indoors when the doorbell rang. It was Sylvia, Joy's sister. She appeared rather agitated, so I invited her in and made her a cup of tea and introduced her to Jason.

'This is an unexpected visit,' I remarked.

'Yes,' she said, 'I had to come and see you. I am very worried about Joy she is in a terrible state.'

'I know, I understand she has lost everything to the boyfriend she had,' I said.

'Yes that's right but she does not know who to turn to for help, I've done my best to console her but it's not enough,' replied Sylvia.

'You realise that as I have certain matters that have to be resolved through the courts with Joy, I am the one person who cannot help her,' I said forcibly.

I looked at Jason and then at Sylvia. I noticed Sylvia had hung her head down in despair and Jason had listened intently to the conversation.

'No you may not be able to elp Rick, but I can,' urged Jason.

Both Sylvia and I looked at Jason, who by now had developed a broad smile.

'Can you Jason. Can you really help?' begged Sylvia.

'I can only try,' replied Jason. On that answer Sylvia jumped off out of her seat and went over to Jason and gave him a hug.

'Don't smother me woman. Look you've put lipstick all over me now. Just give me his full name and last known address, plus anything else you know about im, like his parent's address or car number,' requested Jason.

'I can give you his car number and full name which is Harold Wentworth,' answered Sylvia, 'but that is the only information I have.'

'That'll do for a start,' confirmed Jason, 'I'll get a few of my lads onto it straight away. You'll be amazed at what they can do.'

It seemed that the underworld had their own set of rules and laws where nothing was insurmountable. I had never experienced anything like this first hand before. Nothing appeared to be beyond their powers of detection and dealing with a problem which in this case was going to be covered by an underworld group of vigilantes.

After Sylvia had left the house, I put a few questions to Jason.

'Are you sure you can pull this one off?' I asked.

'Fairly certain,' he confirmed, 'although it might need a few powers of gentle persuasion!'

Two weeks after Joy's visit, Jason received a letter which he handed to me to read. It was from Joy and read:-

Dear Jason,

> *I cannot thank you enough for the help that you had given. Although I did not get all the money returned to me that was taken, I did at least get about seventy five percent back.*
>
> *I don't know what you and your friends did, but it worked wonders. I will be forever grateful and will always remember the help and kindness you offered to me. This is a valuable lesson I have learnt. I shall of course be a bit more careful with my money in the future. Its return will help me fight the action that Rick is putting before the courts, which I have every intention of winning.*

Many thanks once again. Enclosed is the two thousand pounds agreed for the successful outcome.

Regards

Joy

I was staggered by Joy's letter and horrified that my lodger's well meaning intention was going to work against me. Jason was not pleased either and apologised.

'I'm sorry mate the whole thing has backfired on you. I had no idea that she would use this against you,' said Jason.

'You don't know Joy. In fact the sooner I am rid of her, the better I will like it, but the only problem is that divorces can take a long time to get to court,' I replied.

Although at first I didn't like the idea of Jason living with me, I had become used to him being there. He had in fact turned out to be good company, although I had to admit by helping Joy he had messed up badly.

'I notice that events move very quickly in your world Jason. Did you get any feed back on what happened? I asked.

'Oh yes,' said Jason, 'my man soon found this Harold Wentworth. He managed to track him down through his vehicle registration number. Mind you, we had to use a few methods of persuasion. Nothing too drastic you understand. Just some removal of finger nails with the aid of some pliers. Apparently Wentworth held out quite well, because my man only managed to remove six of the ten finger nails before he came round to our way of thinking and handed over a cheque.'

Jason's explanation described in infinite detail made me wince at every description of torture adopted to obtain a satisfactory result.

'Couldn't he have gone to the bank the next day and cancelled the cheque?' I asked.

'Now Rick, that would have been very silly. You don't know the man who confronted im and do you really think Wentworth would like to lose a few more finger nails,' replied Jason with a chuckle.

'Yes, but couldn't he have gone to the Police about being bullied? After all he had not broken the law. He was merely drawing money out of his own joint account,' I pointed out.

'True, and that is why he wouldn't have been roughed up too badly. I would be very surprised if the little worm had not told the old bill. But my man is nameless and faceless because he would have approached Wentworth wearing a disguise and therefore unlikely that he would ever be caught,' indicated Jason. 'In fact this man is so good at covering his tracks, that he is not known to the old bill and hasn't even got a police record,' Jason continued.

I was in awe of how the underworld had achieved their own set of laws and punishments which they enforced decisively and quickly at the same time keeping one step ahead of the police. Despite the effectiveness of Jason's friends I didn't feel that this was an ideal method of enforcing justice.

Chapter 16 Disaster at Home

That night I was mulling over in my mind the recent events surrounding Joy and having great difficulty in sleeping, when I heard the smoke alarm going off. I opened the bedroom door to go downstairs and was confronted with a blast of smoke. I shielded my nose with a damp face flannel and headed for the staircase.

I looked down the stairwell and noticed that the whole of the ground floor hallway was on fire and smoke was billowing everywhere. The heat was so intense it drove me back into the bedroom. Retreating to the ensuite off the bedroom, I doused myself with cold water in readiness to evacuate the building.

I thought of Jason and wondered if he was awake and aware that the house was on fire. I ran out of the bedroom covering my face with a damp cloth, along the corridor. The heat was more intense than the first time I ventured into the corridor and there were signs of flames burning the floor I was standing on. I had to get away from this area quickly and burst into Jason's room. This was full of smoke but Jason appeared to be sleeping though in complete oblivion and I was surprised that the smoke alarm had not wakened him. A brief shake of Jason's shoulder and he was on his feet coughing uncontrollably as smoke enveloped his large frame.

'Jason, the house is on fire, we've got to get out of here,' I screamed at him. 'We can't go down the stairs so we will have to climb out of the window and jump into the garden.'

Jason opened the bedroom door leading into the corridor only to be greeted by a wall of flame. He quickly slammed closed the door. I could see that the flames had reached Jason's bedroom and noticed that Jason's door was slowly being demolished with flames and it wouldn't be long before the whole bedroom was ablaze. Jason then went into his ensuite doused a towel with water and wrapped it around him.

I opened Jason's window ready to make a jump and noticed a person running away from the house with a large container in his hand. In the darkness I could not make out who it was. However it did confirm that the fire was almost certainly a deliberate arson attack. I leaned forward to try and get a better view, but again could not conclude any discerning features of my aggressor. Within seconds he had disappeared behind the trees and away.

Looking down out of the window I realised that the jump to the ground was approximately thirteen feet. This was a big jump to the ground and I contemplated what injuries I could sustain once I hit the ground. While I was wasting time mulling over my thoughts, the flames had taken the bedroom door and moved into the bedroom and could hear breaking glass. I could feel the intense heat on my back and knew that I had no alternative than to make the leap. With one exerted push I had made the jump and came crashing down to the ground with a heavy thump. A sharp pain went though my ankles as I hit the ground. Standing up immediately, I hobbled a few feet away from the building, also to check that I had no broken bones. Checking myself over, I seemed to be alright regarding no broken bones, although the experience did provide me with a sprained ankle when I landed awkwardly and left me hobbling about.

Meanwhile Jason was screaming in pain at the top of his voice. It was obvious he was suffering with the intensity of the heat behind him, which must have vastly increased since my leaving the burning building.

'Jump,' I shouted to Jason. He was uncertain about making the leap to safety, however I could see the flames licking his back, which made the decision for him to release himself from the inferno easier. His overly large body hit the ground with a tremendous thud. I could see he was in agony. His pyjama jacket had burnt from his back which revealed serious burn marks. The back of his head was also burnt badly and he was rolling around in pain holding his leg.

'Rick, I've broken my leg,' he shouted as he rolled from side to side on the ground.

'I'll get an ambulance and the fire brigade here, but you must lay still,' I said dialling the emergency number.

Within ten minutes the fire service had arrived and commenced extinguishing the fire. After another five minutes the ambulance service arrived and had taken the injured Jason to hospital.

Approximately four hours after the fire brigades arrival the uniformed men had managed to quell and eventually put out the fire. The visible damage was heart breaking. Not only had I lost all my possessions but the whole interior of the house and the roof had been completely destroyed. I could see remnants of my possessions smouldering in the building. The adjacent garage had also suffered from the inferno and the car that it housed had also been completely destroyed, leaving the smell of burning rubber tyres filling the air.

For the moment I had to put my sentiments to one side and see Jason in hospital. By the time I had arrived Jason's leg was in plaster and they had given him a drug to dull the pain from the burns he had received on his back and the rear of his head. Jason seemed pleased to see me and greeted me with a smile.

'Have you any idea who would have done this?' Jason asked. He was obviously keen to get even with the perpetrator.

'No, I haven't,' I replied.

'Do you have any enemies who would love to get some revenge?' Jason queried.

'Well, there may be a few possibilities, but more to the point who have you got as enemies?' I asked.

'Oh, I've got quite a few, but they all know better than to cross with me. So we are back to who would want to do you some harm?' insisted Jason.

'The possibilities I'm thinking of is Peter Brown, who thinks I murdered his son and Harold Wentworth, Joy's boyfriend, who Zach went to see. I'm sure he would want to get even in some way, even though Zach thought otherwise,' I confirmed.

'You realise Rick that while I'm in ere, I can not protect you from these nutters,' Jason advised.

Jason was right, up till now I had enjoyed the benefit of a free private bodyguard without realising it. There were several reasons why someone would want to hunt me down, but the main ones surrounded court cases and my unexpected good fortune.

Now that I had no home in which to return, I had to decide where I was going to live while my house was being repaired and recompensed by the insurance company. I thought it might be a good idea to return to Bournemouth and the safety of Janice's Guest House.

Chapter 17 Back at the Guest House

It was great to return to the Guest House. In a funny kind of way, I missed the old place and Janice's friendly banter. Janice was delighted to see me again and gave me a big hug.

'I thought once you left here and went to live in that huge mansion of yours that I would not see you again,' Janice remarked.

'Its good to be back and see you again, but if I'm being honest I am only here because circumstances have dictated my return,' I replied.

I gave Janice a full rundown of the events that had occurred after leaving the Guest House. Janice listened intently intermittently making short gasps as I related some of the unwelcome visitors I received.

'Gosh,' she remarked, 'you have been living on the edge. Still you should be safe here.'

Janice's comforting remarks put me at my ease and I was able to settle in a comfortable chair with a glass of wine and read a newspaper.

My minutes of comfort were not long when I heard a voice call out 'Wallace?'

'Yes, that's me,' I said as I spun round in my chair unhappy that my period of peaceful satisfaction had been disturbed.

'I thought you might still be here,' remarked the spokesman.

I peered over my reading glasses and was shocked to see the large frame of Peter Brown in front of me.

'Come, I want to talk to you outside,' said Brown.

'I think I'd rather stay here,' I answered, doubtful of his intentions.

'It would be in your interests if you did not argue, but were to do as I say,' insisted Brown.

Intrigued, I removed myself from the chair and followed Brown outside, not knowing what to expect.

'Right, my car is over there, I want you to come with me,' insisted Brown.

I looked in the direction to which Brown was pointing and noticed that no one else was in the vehicle but the car door was slightly ajar.

'I don't think so,' I said in resistance and quickly turned about to return to the Guest House.

'You will do as I tell you,' pressed Brown. With that instruction and to my complete surprise, Brown produced a small handgun and pushed it forcefully into the side of my body. I looked around, hoping that there was another person or people about who I could call out to for assistance. Alas, there was no one.

'Don't be a fool Peter,' I insisted and put that gun away.

'Nothing will happen if you follow my instructions. You will go over to my car and you will go quietly,' said Peter pressing the gun further into my back, but shielding the weapon from public gaze by the flap on his overcoat.

Fearful of what he had in mind, I did exactly as he asked. I was in no position to argue with him having been confronted with a hand weapon. When he placed me in the car, to my surprise he clipped a pair of handcuffs on me and restrained me to the seat with the aid of ropes. Having secured me tightly within the vehicle, I tried to think of ways to escape my maniac capturer, but realised that there was nothing I could do.

He drove off at speed which was so fast that I was being thrown in my tethered state from one side of the car to the other collecting many bruises on the way. Protesting all the time at the way I was being treated, he didn't stop until we reached Southampton.

When the car did come to a halt, I noticed that I was in familiar surroundings. It was a wooded area and to my horror realised that it was the same place that I had buried Ralph.

'Get out of the car,' ordered Peter indicating with the barrel of his gun.

I did as he said.

'Are you going to shoot me?' I asked.

'Shoot you? said Peter sadistically, 'No that will be too easy for you. I intend to make you suffer in the same way you made my son suffer.'

'Come on,' ordered Peter as he pushed me with the butt of the gun, 'go down there.'

I looked to where he was pointing and saw a grating on the ground which he carefully removed.

'No! You can't put me underground,' I argued.

'Can't I? Just watch me,' he insisted.

Peter removed the ropes and handcuffs which exposed a redness on the wrists from the chafing. He then supported the lid of the grating and directed me to go through the narrow opening which would take me underground. The dread of what awaited me by allowing myself to follow his instructions filled me with intense fear. A nudge in my back from the barrel of a gun persuaded me to do as he asked. With one hand of Peter's supporting the lid and with the other hand pushing my body, I was manhandled to descend into this den of horror. Looking around I had noticed that the hole was approximately six feet by six feet and four feet in height. There was some food placed in the corner of the den. Against all my protestations Peter ignored my rantings, returned the grating and filled over the top of it with soil. I heard and shuddered at every spade of clay thudding on the grating in the course of the backfilling. Then came the moment which I was dreading when I was submerged almost in complete darkness.

There appeared to be a small amount of light coming from a four inch diameter tube. On the floor of the hole was a carpet to which I could hardly believe my eyes. It was a red carpet displaying a blue fluorescent diamond similar to the one that Joy had bought, albeit on a smaller scale. This evil gesture of Peter's was strategically placed there evidently to sadistically remind me of that terrible night. Peter then started to speak to me via the only piece of apparatus where contact could be made, through the air tube.

'You are now interred in the same way that you buried my son except I have afforded you more room than the space you gave him. I thought you might feel at home with the decorative carpet I have left you. After all, you did leave a similar patterned carpet with my son's grave. There is sufficient food and water to last you for three days, after that you have nothing and you will not be receiving any further supplies. My aim is to make you suffer for what you did to my son, so it was never my intention to give you the benefit of a quick death. That would be too easy,' said Peter with some relish in his voice.

I leant forward to the air tube so that I could speak to him and saw it as my last chance to persuade him and make him see the foolishness of his actions by appealing to the better side of his nature.

'Why are you doing this Peter when you have a court case against me pending? I asked.

'Oh that's just a diversionary tactic, the authorities would never think that I would get rid of you if I stood to make a lot of money, so as you can see I never intended to go through the court case at all,' admitted Peter.

'Peter, I beg you. You have nothing to gain by doing this,' I pleaded.

'Well, I'm going to leave you to your solitude now and I won't be back, goodbye,' confirmed Peter.

'Wait! Wait! Don't leave me' I shouted, but there was no reply.

I was left in this eerie den of dampness, darkness, silence and in a completely distressed state of mind. Although I was hungry, I didn't dare touch any of the food which was in the corner of the hole, I had to eek this out for as long as possible. With tremendous effort and within the limited room that I had, I tried to lift the lid of the cast iron grating, but there was too much soil holding it down, making this idea of a quick escape not viable.

After two hours, nightfall came removing the small beam of light I was receiving from the air hole. I noticed also by the droplets of water coming from the air hole that it was raining heavily. The den started to fill up with water and it wasn't long before the carpet I was sitting on was submerged under two inches of water. I had to do something quick about the food as I didn't want it to rot under such wet conditions, so I turned the water canister on its side and balanced the food carefully on the top. Also I managed to balance some food on top of the chemical toilet which Peter Brown had thoughtfully included for my use.

My discomfort was such that I couldn't sleep. Every part of me had started to ache through the wet and cramped conditions. The night was the longest I had ever known and when the morning came and shone a small ray of light into the den through the air tube, it seemed like a small relief. However there were problems which I was faced with that had to be addressed. The wet floor was giving me a painful cramp in the legs so I had to get rid of the water that I was sitting in. I dug away at the ground with my bare hands so that I was able to make a small sump for the water to escape in the corner of the den.

Being left alone to my thoughts was having a disastrous effect on me, as I pondered about the impossible situation I was in. I kept thinking to myself 'will anyone ever find me, or if they don't find me alive will they find me when I'm dead?'

I started eating the food which was some fruit a few uncooked vegetables and some sliced beef. I counted what was there and divided it into sufficient portions to last me a week. Every day I would do some exercises to try and relieve my aching limbs, although the cramped conditions afforded me little movement. The only way I could stretch out was to lie down, but even in this stretched position it brought a problem of dampness in direct contact with my skin. I came to the conclusion that the cramped location provided no ideal comfort no matter what position was adopted.

Another night came then another day. The nights were cold and I could do nothing to keep myself warm. If it rained I started to find a way to use the elements to my advantage, by putting the nozzle of the water canister under the air pipe to catch the drops, which I would then use as drinking water.

Periodically I would call out through the air hole, hoping that someone would hear me and release me from my plight which became more difficult to endure as time went by.

Spreading the food over more days meant that I was only getting less than a fifty percent sustenance which made me feel very weak and by the seventh day I had completely used up all my rations.

On day eight I was living off worms and the rare beetles that found themselves at the sides of the den. I only had sufficient water because of the occasional rainfall. Even the dirty rainwater that had found its way into the sump, I resorted to use when my supplies had become scarce.

On day nine, the water canister was completely empty and due to the unreliability of the wet weather, I could no longer rely on rain drops entering the den to assist my thirst. I had resigned myself to succumb to death in the den and lay on the sodden carpet just waiting for this to happen. I had completely run out of food and even the worms were in short supply. Then for the first time during my captivity I could here children playing outside. In my weakened state I shouted as loud as I could though the air tube, hoping that my sounds of distress would be heard. Then everything went quiet. I shouted again and this time to my delight I received a response.

'Who are you and what are you doing underground?' came the voice of what appeared to be from an adult.

'I am Richard Wallace and I am the victim of a kidnap, please help me, I have been here in captivity for over a week,' I replied.

'Just hold on for approximately an hour, I have to get a spade and then I will get you out of there,' came the same voice. Then there was a deathly silence. I had started to give up hope thinking that the offer of help may have been a sadistic hoax instigated by Peter Brown and therefore would not materialise. It was therefore a surprise that true to his word my helper returned. I could hear the digging going on above me, then eventually the pleasing sound of the grating creaking as it was being lifted, darting a stream of sunlight into the den. I looked up and saw about four people, but could not identify any of their features, because the sudden rush of light was having an effect on my eyes. I tried to shield my eyes from the light with my grubby hands and gradually tried to accustom them to the brightness by widening the cracks between my fingers.

My helpers reached down and pulled me up. When I reached the safety of the surface, I found that I had lost the use of my muscles in the legs. Although it was of no surprise, I could tell by my skeletal form that I had lost a lot of weight.

When my eyes had become more accustomed to the light I was able to distinguish my helpers as being three policemen together with the man who had discovered my whereabouts. He was a young man about twenty three years of age, approximately five feet ten inches in height and called himself Robert.

'Who did this to you?' one of the officers asked.

'Peter Brown,' I answered.

'Who is Peter Brown. Do you know him?' he questioned.

'Oh yes, I know him well and I can tell you where he lives,' I replied trying to brush the dirt off my very wet clothes.

'Are you prepared to detail your ordeal and testify against Peter Brown?' asked the officer.

'Yes, indeed I am,' I replied.

'Thank you. That will be the last time you will be troubled by this man,' the officer assured as he frantically wrote down the answers to my questions.

Robert gave me a cheese sandwich which I snatched from his hand and devoured like some gluttonous Neanderthal man who had just happened to have stumbled on a piece of meat. He then gave me some hot tea from a flask which I treated with equal impatience. After I finished feeding and drinking, I apologised to Robert for my strange behaviour which he treated with complete understanding.

One of the officers left armed with the information I had given him and shortly afterwards the ambulance turned up. The three remaining men had to carry me into the vehicle and I was transported to the same hospital where Jason was located for treatment. Luckily after a nice hot bath and something to eat, I was placed in the same ward as Jason, who witnessed, to his apparent delight, my arrival.

Jason immediately hobbled over and spoke to me.

'What happened to you?' You look so thin, you look terrible,' he observed.

'Oh, I've been living like a mole for the last few days and I don't recommend it,' I remarked. I then went on to explain what had happened to me in the intervening period between the last day that I saw Jason and now.

'I wondered why you hadn't come in to see me,' Jason remarked. 'Would you like me to see what I can do to make this geaser think that he had made a big mistake?'

'No, that's not necessary, my friends the boys in blue are taking care of matters now,' I confirmed.

After three days of treatment and learning how to walk again I was discharged from hospital leaving Jason behind for further treatment.

Two days later I went back to the hospital to see Jason.

'Tell me,' he said, 'did you ever find out the name of the person who torched the house?'

'I hadn't given it a great deal of thought as my mind has been occupied on how to stay alive,' I replied.

'Do you think it might have been that Brown feller who kidnapped you?' asked Jason.

'That is very unlikely, because he didn't even know that I had moved from the Guest House. It was just my bad luck that I moved back on the same day he was looking for me,' I responded.

'Then it must have been Harold Wentworth,' concluded Jason. 'Do you want one of my guys to pay him a little visit. We know where he lives now.'

'No, that won't be necessary, I will look into it as soon as I get back from the hospital,' I assured Jason.

When I returned to the Guest House I phoned the fire service and enquired if they had reached any conclusions regarding the house fire. I was informed that they had made out a report and passed all their findings to the police department. I decided to pay the boys in blue a visit to see if they had also discovered anything. I gave my name to the officer at the desk.

'We've been looking for you,' said the desk officer.

'Can you give me any information regarding the fire?' I enquired.

'Yes,' he confirmed 'we are satisfied that it was started deliberately, so we are looking at a crime of arson.'

'How did you reach that conclusion?' I asked.

'There was a smell of petrol in the hallway indicating that fuel had been poured in through the letterbox followed by something like a match or taper that would have ignited the gasoline,' came the reply.

'I do have close circuit surveillance at home, but I don't know if it was destroyed in the fire,' I said.

'That would be helpful, but have you any idea who would want to do this to you?' asked the officer.

'I do have my suspicions, but first I would like to return back to the house to see what I can find,' I replied.

Leaving the police station I made my way back to my house. It did look a sorry state with most of the windows broken, some obvious vandalism and opportunist theft since the fire. I checked the lounge where my close circuit equipment was operating. The equipment although smoke damaged was fine, so I rewound and played back the tape. I almost fell asleep waiting for some movement on the screen, then I noticed a man with a petrol can appearing from behind the trees. Then he disappeared out of the range of the camera, which meant that I was unable to get a glimpse of his face.

After a few minutes the whole of the front garden lit up from the glare of the fire and then the camera picked up my intruder running off carrying his petrol can. He then stopped running and turned round to look at his handiwork. It was at this moment I was able to get a good look at his face. Yes, my suspicions were correct it was unmistakably Harold Wentworth.

Thrilled to bits with my detective work and ultimate discovery I gave my information to the police, together with Wentworth's car number which would lead them to the home address.

It was time to visit Jason to see if his health was improving and updating him on current events and the manner they were being dealt with. Jason would have called this 'pay back time'.

Chapter 18 Visit to Jason

At the hospital, Jason did look a sorry state. The burns he received did nothing to enhance his appearance which was the scary look of a hardened thug. However he didn't seem too concerned that his facial features had changed most distinctively for the worst. His view was that if anything this would help his general style of achieving what he wanted from people though the process of sheer fear. His leg was still in plaster and he was walking with the aid of crutches. When I informed him that Wentworth had started the fire, he wanted to engage his henchmen to teach him a lesson. It was all I could do but to persuade him to leave well alone and let the police deal with it, however I did advise that if he did require some retribution, then he could attain this by putting in a claim against Wentworth for the injuries he had sustained.

'You seem to be managing very well without me and doing everything legally by the book,' admitted Jason.

It seemed that whatever Jason did, it did not include legal representation or assistance so he seemed quite surprised that I had managed to sort things out with a calculated law abiding aptitude.

'Tell me Jason are you always trying to sort problems out and seeking retribution against people that do you wrong?'

'Pretty much so,' replied Jason.

'I must admit that I am finding that I am living a similar lifestyle to you at the moment with problems occurring one after the other in close succession. I am not sure that I can cope with it in the same way you do,' I confided.

'Oh, you do get used to it after a while, also you learn how to deal with problems. The main thing is not to weaken or let it get you down,' advised Jason.

'That's easy for you to say, everything is happening so fast, I keep wondering what is going to hit me next,' I replied.

'Well I can tell you what is coming next, I shall be released from ere in three days time,' revealed Jason, 'but what do I do about living accommodation?'

'When you are discharged by the doctor, make your way to the Guest House where I am staying in Bournemouth,' I advised.

True to his word, when the three days had elapsed Jason appeared at the Guest House, his leg in plaster and struggling to carry his large frame on his crutches. However his injuries didn't make him miserable or affect his disposition in anyway. If anything he would chuckle about his ailments and found it a regular source of conversation.

Six months later I received notification that my house originally damaged by fire, had undergone repairs and was ready to move back into. By this time Jason had dispensed with his leg plaster and crutches.

It was spring when we moved back to the house and both of us were looking forward to a bright and trouble free future. I had every reason to believe this, because the two people that were previously giving me cause for concern, Harold Wentworth and Peter Brown were both doing long spells in prison.

The house had been restored to its former glory. It was impossible to detect that substantial fire damage had ever taken place. I bought all new furniture and had great fun filling the home with everything I liked and enjoyed.

It was pleasing to see Jason joining me as my usual regular lodger. Pleasing because not only was he good company, I saw myself as a target by many people and felt safe when he was around.

I hadn't been back a month when the door bell rang. Old habits die hard, so I continued my usual practice of peering through the side window to see who was calling. There were two men who I didn't know, so I called out to Jason.

'Yes, I was expecting these two men. It's okay, let them in,' said Jason.

Apprehensively I opened the door. To my surprise Jason's two callers rudely pushed past me without saying a word. One of them was a small man approximately five foot four inches in height, in his early twenties and the other was approximately six feet tall in his late thirties. The smaller man had fair hair and a scar on his cheek and the older man had jet black hair with two large warts on his face, one on the tip of his nose and one on his chin. I began to think that Jason had got the ugliest collection of friends I had ever seen.

'Rick I would like you to meet two of my very dear friends,' said Jason.

I extended my hand to the older man who did not want to reciprocate the handshake, so I turned to the smaller man who responded in the same discourteous manner.

'This is Albert,' said Jason pointing to the smaller man, 'and this is Godfrey,' he added pointing to the larger of the two.

The three men huddled together in the lounge and became heavily engrossed in conversation. I left them to it, believing that whatever they were talking about it was better that I didn't get involved.

After an hour of deep discussion, Jason came looking for me.

'Come into the lounge, we have a few things to discuss which involves you,' said Jason.

I didn't know what Jason was talking about, but my curiosity allowed me to follow his instructions. When I arrived in the lounge and selected a seat to sit on, I noticed my two unsociable visitors could not take their eyes off me. The manner of these two men staring at me during a moment of eerie silence was making me feel uncomfortable. Then the silence was broken by Jason.

'Rick we need your help,' said Jason.

'Well I'll do what I can,' I responded.

'I know I can rely on your absolute discretion,' said Jason, 'so that is why I have come to you.'

I looked at the three of them not knowing what was coming next.

'Look Rick, I'm not going to beat about the bush. We are in the process of making plans to do a bank job and would appreciate your elp,' said Jason in a voice which was so innocuous with his information you would have thought that he was telling me of an intended holiday or similar, rather than an involvement in a serious crime.

'Jason I do not want to get involved,' I replied immediately and firmly.

'I haven't told you what we want you to do yet,' said Jason.

'Do you want me to sort im out?' said Godfrey who stood up and menacingly walked over to me. 'It's obvious that you can't trust im.'

'No! Sit down Godfrey,' said Jason. Godfrey did as he was told and Jason then turned his attention on me again.

'Rick. All we wonna do is use your gaff to meet up after the job and divide and split the booty,' confirmed Jason.

'I must admit I'm not happy about it. Is it really necessary to resort to crime?' I remarked.

'Well how else do yer think I get dosh for me board and lodging to stay ere,' replied Jason.

'I'm sorry Jason if you do this crime and use my place for your ill-gotten gains,' it is not with my consent.

'I understand, then we'll do it without your consent,' insisted Jason.

Our conversation having expired, it was time for Jason's visitors to leave. I must confess I wasn't sorry to see the back of them and hoped that they would not return. They never gave me the courtesy of appreciation for the hospitality of my house and never said goodbye. I wasn't sure what Jason was going to do, having vetoed any idea of him using my house for the dividing of the spoils, but whatever he decided I intended to distance myself from it.

One week later Jason advised me not to return to the house on Tuesday next between the hours of one and four o'clock, saying he preferred to keep the reason secret. I believed I had a rough idea why he wanted to be alone in the house and complied with his wishes without question. He was obviously ignoring the veto I had placed on him.

Although I was not happy to be turned out of my own house on Tuesday, I was pleased that I was not involved in any of the crimes or double dealings that these three gangsters were engaged in and therefore saw it as a blessing in disguise. After all I couldn't be implicated over something that I was unaware. I was therefore pleased when Tuesday came and went. However I noticed when I returned home that Jason was not his usual happy self. Had everything gone wrong with their well thought out plans? I was frightened to ask and acted as though it was a normal day.

I wasn't left in a state of curiosity for long because my daily newspaper revealed the true horror that happened. Contents of the tabloid read as follows:-

> *A gang of three masked men broke into a bank in Bournemouth yesterday and stole approximately seven hundred thousand pounds. The men were armed and shot bank*

clerk Leonard Williams at close range in the chest after he would not submit to their demands. He is currently in a coma at the Accident and Emergency hospital where he is fighting for his life. Mr. Williams is married with two children. His wife is offering a reward to anyone that leads to the capture of the perpetrator of this crime. It is believed that the heist was committed by local men.

Police are asking for any witnesses to this incident to come forward with any information they may have.

I didn't need to read anymore of the detail. I was now placed in an invidious position of knowing who the gangsters were. For although I tried to distance myself from the crime, I realised that by media circulation of information and request for knowledge, I had become unwittingly a crucial witness to this dreadful encounter. I was implicated before, during and after the incident. I looked at Jason who was sleeping in the chair as if he hadn't got a care in the world.

'What's the meaning of this?' I shouted at Jason kicking his feet to get his attention from his slumber and at the same time throwing the newspaper at him.

Jason woke with a startled look of surprise, grabbed the paper and started to read what I had pushed under his nose. As he perused the contents, I saw for the very first time a look of concern on his face.

'Oh dear,' he said as he read the contents.

'How did you come to shoot someone?' I pressed Jason.

'I didn't shoot anyone and it wasn't my fault. One of the bank clerks thought he would have a go and hot headed Godfrey shot im at point blank range, because he refused to hand over the dosh,' revealed Jason.

'Why did you find it necessary to carry guns in the first place?' I asked angrily.

'The guns were only implements to create fear, they weren't intended to be used,' protested Jason.

'But you did use them and if this man dies, you could all go down for a long stretch and it will serve you all right,' I pointed out.

'Not me,' he said, 'there may be an honour amongst thieves, but not in my case. I will rat on anyone to save my own skin.'

On that last remark of Jason's he gently handed me back the newspaper and went back to sleep.

The news on the evening television brought home to me my worst fears. The unfortunate bank clerk involved in the heist had lost his battle for survival. The police were now looking at a murder enquiry and unfortunately I knew a lot more than I wanted to know.

From then onwards I dreaded anyone ringing the doorbell. I began to wonder whether I should be proactive by informing the police authorities on everything I knew. If it was Alice who had incriminating evidence, I knew she wouldn't hesitate. However the difficulty in acting as an informer brought other problems because I was aware how Jason and his so-called friends in the underworld thought about anyone who grassed them up.

They had their own methods of retribution and mindful of this I valued all my limbs and my health.

Two weeks after the incident my fears were reactivated with a police calling on us. Jason answered the door and the officer was invited in.

'I am looking for the owner of this property,' requested the officer.

'I am the owner,' I confessed.

'There is a car registered to this address under the name of Jason Fairclove. This vehicle was involved as a get-away car in a bank heist. Is that you?' questioned the officer.

This was a surprise. Jason had obviously but carelessly used his own vehicle in the robbery and had not used false plates, the usual cover up criminals adopt when attempting to retreat in a getaway car.

'No, the car belongs to me,' said Jason stepping forward with his hand up.

'Were you driving this vehicle at around two o'clock in the afternoon exactly fourteen days ago?' quizzed the officer.

'Yes I was,' admitted Jason.

'Then I have to inform you that you are under arrest for the murder of Ian Candy and your involvement in the robbery in the bank at Bournemouth. Anything you say may be used as evidence against you,' said the officer. Jason was then clamped in handcuffs and frogmarched to a waiting police car. As Jason was led away he was trying to protest his innocence regarding the murder of the bank clerk.

Two days later I received another visit from the police.

'Were you involved in the Bank robbery in Bournemouth,' asked the officer.

'No, I was not,' I answered nervously.

'Can you prove that?' asked the officer.

'Yes, I confirmed I was having a few drinks with some friends on the day in question in the Red Lion. The Publican will verify my story,' I replied.

'Good,' said the officer, 'what do you know about the robbery and killing of a bank clerk Ian Candy.'

This was a difficult one to answer because although I wasn't directly involved, Jason had volunteered me all the information.

'Well mostly what I read in the newspaper,' I replied 'you will have to get the information from Jason Fairclove.'

'He has already informed us who shot the gun that fatally killed the bank clerk,' said the officer, 'but did you know anything about the robbery?'

I was relieved to have learnt that Jason had made a confession about the killing.

'Then I have nothing to add,' I answered.

'Thank you sir, I will check out your alibi with the publican and if it corroborates with the story you have given me, then you will hear no more. I bid you good day,' said the officer and left.

Chapter 19 My New Friend

Two weeks later I learnt that Godfrey had been charged with the murder of the bank clerk and was serving life imprisonment. Jason and Albert had been charged with robbery and was serving a six year jail term each.

The empty house brought mixed feelings about Jason's departure. Although I missed the company I saw his departure as fortuitous blessing in disguise, because I had started to believe that many of my problems emanated from his heavy handed approach to life, his principles of revenge on the unfortunates that got in the way and frustrated his unconventional ways of living.

For the next two months everything seemed serene compared with the hectic life full of multiple problems I was forced to endure since that fateful day, when I was woken up by Joy to deal with an intruder in the house. In fact life became so uneventful, that I had become lethargic and the ennui that set in as a direct result of my laziness, encouraged me to break away from the regular pattern of home life and take a job.

After some searching I managed to find a building site locally and applied for a job as a bricklayer. The interviewer was very thorough in his selection of labour as he asked me if I had done decorative face work, embellishments and masonry work. Not content with the questions, he asked me to build a wall size one metre square in decorative face work and timed my progress during its construction. Having satisfied the initial requirements and secured the job through this intense scrutiny, he set me to work with a gang of bricklayers.

The contract was behind time, so the bonuses were good and there was opportunity to do overtime. Within my gang there was a man who was the same age as me called Herbert Long. I immediately struck up a friendship with this man who in many ways was very similar to myself. He had the same jet black hair and was of the same height. Our likenesses were so exact that we could have been taken for identical twins. In fact it became difficult for the foreman to tell us apart. For our amusement we liked to add to the confusion by wearing similar clothes in style and colour.

Herbert liked to be called 'Bert'. I found that the annals of my life experiences appeared to have had an effect on me, because in order for me to strike up a friendship, I had to ascertain that the person was of good character, had not been involved in any form of crime and indeed had honourable intentions. In the days that past and by the subtle prudence of my questioning, Bert's credentials appeared to tick all the boxes of my strict code of refinement as a decent human being.

Our friendship became such that we would meet up socially sometimes after work. We would also play pranks on one another like swapping a colleagues trowel over with one which had the handle purposely weakened with a rasp, so that it would break in two when attempting to snap a header or cut a brick closer. This would bring about fits of laughter from the other members of the gang.

Then one day something happened that changed everything around and had a disastrous effect on the friendship. We had gone off for a drink in the local public house a few yards from the building site and was enjoying the usual banter between us, when Bert made an odd remark which needed following up.

'It's rather strange,' he remarked, 'I'm seeing a woman who has the same surname as you and wondered if it could be a relative.'

'What, the name Wallace?' I confirmed.

'Yes, that's right,' he agreed.

'Oh, there are a lot of people of that name, I doubt that it is a relative or anyone I know,' I insisted.

'Her name is Joy. Has a lot of money and not afraid to spend it, also very sexy in bed. Are you sure you don't know her?' asked Bert.

'Is she slim with fair hair,' I queried.

'Yes, that's right. I do believe you do know her after all don't you,' said Bert smiling.

'Oh, I know her alright and yes, she is a relative. She happens to be my wife,' I said sternly.

Bert picked up on the seriousness of the situation, the smile had disappeared from his face and was looking most uncomfortable. He started fidgeting with a beer mat and his face reddened up with embarrassment.

'I'm sorry old man. I had no idea. I don't know what to say,' he bumbled in his obvious contrition.

In an odd kind of way Bert had done me a favour because I started to believe that I could use adultery as my main reason for divorcing Joy instead of desertion. This meant that I could dispel with the lengthy period that desertion offered in obtaining a divorce in favour of my speedier newly found alternative. Bert had unwittingly found himself in the middle of a divorce action.

'I think I'd better go home,' said Bert, still feeling in his embarrassment as though his whole world had collapsed.

I didn't answer but watched Bert down the rest of his pint of beer in one gulp and slowly vacate the Public House as if he was in some kind of trance, leaving me on my own. I knew then that I had lost a dear friend as

I could hardly mention his name to obtain a decree nisi and still remain his constant companion.

The following day Bert approached the Foreman and tendered his notice of termination and left the workplace straight away without offering any reason for his sudden departure to his employer or any farewell to me. I was glad that he had done this, because if he hadn't taken that course of action, then I would have felt it a duty to end my employment as I couldn't have continued a close working relationship with him.

It was time to contact Alice to catch up on what was happening against the action I was taking against Joy.

'I'm glad you have come to see me,' said Alice, 'I was going to contact you.'

'Well I have a bit of information to give you,' I said. I related to her the revelation offered by my building friend and suggested she progressed the divorce quickly, using my latest offering of damning information.

'You may not be aware, but the law has changed and unless Long was the cause of your breakup, he can not actually be named,' confirmed Alice.

'Well he wasn't the cause of Joy leaving me so that has ruined that idea,' I replied.

'Don't worry the time will go by quicker than you think,' advised Alice.

'What is happening about getting Joy to court with a view to getting my name vindicated,' I asked Alice.

'I'm still working on obtaining a slot in court, but will let you know as soon as I am informed,' Alice replied.

'However there is something else I want to talk to you about Rick which is quite unrelated. We are now in the leap year 2004 and as a woman, it entitles me to use my prerogative to ask you for a date,' requested Alice.

'Oh, I not sure that is a good idea, both of us are married,' I said.

'Rick, you don't understand I'm not taking 'No' for an answer, so you can forget all negatives. Regarding my marriage that you just mentioned, I like you am seeking a divorce.

'Well Alice, as you will only accept an answer in the affirmative, I had better comply without any further complaint,' I replied with a smile. In accepting Alice's offer I had to forget the problems of the past when she informed the police about my involvement with Ralph Brown and instead concentrate on the best times I had shared with Alice the last time we were together.

Chapter 20 Meeting up with Alice again

It was great meeting up with Alice again. Our date was so successful that in hindsight I was pleased that Alice had asked me to go on a night out. We spent part of the evening at an Italian restaurant and followed this up in the Festival Hall in London listening to a Mozart orchestral movement. Then it was back to her house for coffee, biscuits and a long chat on what had happened since we last met. I also quizzed Alice on her pastimes and what she liked doing most.

'I love sailing,' said Alice.

'Do you have a boat?' I asked.

'Yes, I have a small sixteen foot sailing boat which I keep in the garden. Do you like sailing Rick?' enquired Alice.

'I would if I was better at it. I tend to set off somewhere and end up where I started,' I replied.

'Well surely that's the way it should be, because there is a need to come back to your trailer or mooring,' Alice pointed out.

'I suppose you're right but not if there is a need for you to be rescued and brought back to your starting point,' I answered.

'Tell you what we will do, next Saturday if the weather is fine, we will go out in my boat for the day,' Alice suggested.

'I'd rather we didn't,' I replied.

'Oh, Rick, you will never make a sailor,' said Alice.

I chuckled to myself at her last remark, not daring to tell her of the experience I had when I tried to escape from the country.

We had so much to talk about and time went rapidly by without me noticing it.

'Gosh, look at the time' I said as I noticed that it was three o'clock in the morning, 'and I've got work today, I have to be there at eight o'clock.'

I quickly grabbed my coat said a brief farewell and was out of the door.

Seeing each other again was the prelude to many more times shared together and it wasn't long before I had asked Alice to move in with me.

Time went by so quickly and before I knew it Alice had been living with me a full nine months and my life had appeared to have settled down for me a bit. However I noticed that Alice never made any attempt to follow up her divorce proceedings. This would have been easy for her because unlike me she had clear grounds for quickly dissolving the marriage due to her husband's infidelity and she was after all in the business at catering for divorce. It was time for me to broach the delicate subject on why she had been so slow in finalising this.

'Alice, I have noticed that you have not been actively seeking to dissolve your marriage,' I commented.

'Yes,' you're right, however I can not see what benefit can be gained by me doing this,' replied Alice.

'Well, it would help to regularise our situation and stabilise the relationship on a firmer footing,' I argued.

'If you mean regularise by the two of us getting married, you must know Rick that can not happen because you are also married,' replied Alice.

Alice was right so I knew I wasn't going to win this one, so I pursued her on another line of questioning.

'Tell me, what is your husband like, is he anything like me?' I quizzed.

'Funnily enough, he is very much like you Rick. You wouldn't believe how alike you both are. In fact it was the similarities that attracted me to him in the first place,' replied Alice.

I was intrigued about what this man had that was similar to me. I wanted to know more and was pleased that Alice didn't mind talking about her husband or her marriage. Finding someone like me could only be a compliment. I was intrigued and continued with my line of questioning.

'In what way is he similar?' I asked.

'Well, he has the exactly the same facial features as you, is the same height, you both have similar personalities and the uncanny thing about it is that he too is a bricklayer,' revealed Alice.

'I notice Alice that you do not use his name, you use still your maiden name,' I commented.

'Yes, that's purely a matter of preference and that's how I like it and want it to remain,' insisted Alice.

'What is his name?' I asked.

'Oh, his name is Long,' said Alice.

I wondered if it was the same person called Long who I had once worked alongside, although this was too much of a coincidence, but I had to ask the question.

'Do you mean Herbert Long?' I asked.

'Yes. You know him don't you Rick,' said Alice with an embarrassed look on her face.

The answer struck me like a bolt from the blue. The full realisation came to me of what my questions had materialised and the stark implication of the situation before me. Alice had left Long as a result of an affair between her husband and my wife. Without me knowing it, we had in fact swopped partners.

'Alice, you were dealing with my divorce, you must have known about Herbert's infidelity with my wife,' I suggested.

'Oh, I knew alright, but there was no point in telling you, because you can't use Herbert's name as a co-respondent in your own action, I have already told you that,' Alice pointed out.

'No, you're probably right. However I think you could have informed me anyway,' I said to Alice in anger.

We continued arguing the point regarding her clandestine approach until I became weary of the subject, when absolute silence between us took over from the sound of busy chatter. We sat staring at one another trying to work out what the other one was thinking. The uncomfortable silence was broken by me.

'Alice, if there is a future for us together, then you must be honest with me. You must not hold any secrets,' I said.

'I'm sorry Rick, I know what you are saying is right. I hope there is a future for us and I shall work hard to make sure that there is,' assured Alice.

These were comforting words from Alice which gave me a warm feeling of reassurance and well being.

Chapter 21 Visiting Jason

Although unpalatable, I thought it was time I paid Jason a visit in prison. In many respects I dreaded returning to the place that held many bad memories for me. When I did get to see my old friend he was delighted to meet up with me again, albeit in the controlled environment under the authorities rules and regulations.

'How are you?' I asked. 'You are certainly looking well,' I commented.

'Yes,' I've settled down quite well in ere,' replied Jason.

'I noted that you were compliant with the police in giving the names of your accomplices in the raid,' I said.

'Yes, I did that for two reasons. Firstly I didn't want to implicate you in any way, and secondly I didn't want to take the rap for that gun happy idiot Godfrey,' revealed Jason.

'Is there anyone you have met up with while you have been in here?' I enquired.

'Yes, there are two of your old friends in here Wentworth and Brown. Brown is doing a twenty year stretch and Wentwoth only six years. That should keep them away from you for a while. Don't worry I'm making their life hell for what they did to you. By the time I've finished with them they'd wished they'd never been born, or at least they'd certainly wished that they had never crossed you,' related Jason.

I looked around the visiting hall and noticed that Dianne Brown was visiting her husband Peter.

As I gazed in their direction, I noticed that Peter with a disapproving look had caught my eye. I quickly turned my attention back to Jason and never looked towards the Browns again.

'That's very thoughtful of you Jason, but go easy on them,' I insisted.

Having known first hand of Jason's capabilities to other inmates who didn't share common views with him, I was quite fearful for their health and any possible retribution directed towards me.

'Is there anything you want me to deal with while I'm in here? I can still make contact with the outside,' confirmed Jason.

'What do you mean?' I asked.

'Well has anyone upset yer? Do you need anyone duffing up? Do you require anyone maimed or a knee capping job done? Jason enquired. 'All can be arranged with the ease of a telephone call to a few of my friends,' he continued.

I sat in my chair squirming uncomfortably at the four ghastly suggestions put forward by Jason, wincing at every method of torture which came out of his mouth, which he not only conveyed with absolute relish, but the words seemed to roll quite naturally off his tongue without any expression of wrongdoing. I recalled to memory also Jason's help in the past which brought about immediate repercussions of devastating retribution against me.

'No thank you Jason,' I confirmed quite convincingly, currently I have everything under control.

'When will you be released from here?' I asked.

'In four years time, if I keep me nose clean and I come up for parole. However I do have an appeal coming up in court, then all being well, I will be back with you before you know it,' Jason said.

This was not what I wanted to hear. The very idea of Jason returning to my home, entertaining gangsters and plotting robberies filled me with awe and I was quick to inform him that there was no chance he could return to where he left off. A realisation came over me that I had to tell him that he could not return to the comforts of my hospitality.

'I'm sorry Jason I have a lady living with me at present and therefore can not acquiesce to your dreams of the future by allowing you a promise of accommodation,' I insisted.

My last remark brought an immediate look of anger from Jason and he quickly grabbed my arm and menacingly drew me closer to him.

'You appear to av a short memory, old boy. Look at what I av done for you in the past, some of which as landed me in ospital,' expressed Jason in annoyance.

This hell raiser was having the successful effect of injecting fear into me. I was beginning to wish that I hadn't made my visit to Jason, felt that I had outstayed my welcome and was looking for a reason to leave. Fortunately the bell rang for visitors to vacate the premises and I was more than ready to make my exit, but as I left Jason called back to me.

'I won't forget this in an urry, you mark my words, you'll be sorry you turned me away,' he yelled.

Jason's threat inflicted a bit of terror in me and knowing him well I could tell by his voice that he was very annoyed at my rebuttal. I was also aware that he very rarely made a threat without carrying it through.

I made my way to the exit door and noticed Dianne Brown immediately following behind me. When I had reached the fresh air of outside the building and prison gates, I quickly walked over to my car, only to find Dianne still close on my heels directly behind me. As I opened the car door, I was stopped by Dianne from entering the vehicle.

'You may have thought you have got away with your crime, but you haven't. I shall make sure of it,' Dianne threatened.

On returning back home, I sought Alice out for a chat on the days events.

'You see now Alice, there is an even greater need to bring this case to court as early as possible because while it is pending there will always be this uncertainty of my guilt,' I urged Alice.

'Well it's odd that you should say that. I have just been informed of a date for a day in court,' advised Alice.

'Well don't keep me in suspense. When is it?' I urged.

'Not until 2nd November,' replied Alice.

'Oh that's wonderful news. That's in only eight and a half week's time,' I said smiling.

'Yes,' she said, 'it just gives us time to prepare our case.'

'Surely there is not much we can do,' I remarked.

'Our main problem is that Joy has a lot of money to engage a top class lawyer, so we must cover every eventuality of what she would probably give in evidence. Rick you know her well. Have you any idea of what she would be likely to say or expose in the case that wasn't previously brought before the courts?' asked Alice.

'I'm sorry, I have no idea. I certainly can not think of anything at the moment, but she could say anything, she is so unpredictable' I replied.

'I will have to refresh myself of the contents of the last case and will let you know if I have any queries or if there is anything outstanding which needs clarifying,' confirmed Alice.

Chapter 22 Problem with Alice

I noticed that since I had the argument with Alice the atmosphere was rather cool between us. In fact she would often leave the house offering no explanation of where she was going or what she was doing. I wasn't sure if her jaunts were for her own entertainment or work related.

Then one day when she left the house, she had forgotten to take her mobile phone with her. Half way into the day the phone rang and I picked it up and answered the call.

'Hello, this is Alice's phone, I'm afraid she is not available at present, but if you give me your details I shall get her to call you back,' I said.

'Just tell her that her husband called. We are meant to be meeting up tonight for dinner but I am not sure of the time that was arranged,' replied the caller.

'I'll inform her and tell her to phone you back,' I confirmed.

I was surprised that the caller did not request who was taking the message. Placed in a quandary, I was clock watching waiting for Alice to return. When she did finally arrive home I started to bombard her with a lot of awkward questions.

'Alice you forgot to take your mobile phone with you. Your husband called your phone today and wants you to ring him back about tonight's arrangements for meeting up,' I informed.

'I'll ring him back in a minute, it's not important,' said Alice looking embarrassed.

'Alice. Are you seeing Herbert Long on a regular basis?' I asked.

'Yes, I have been seeing him form time to time but there again, you have been seeing Joy on the odd occasion,' Alice argued.

I ignored Alice's point about seeing Joy, because I was aware that I was no longer romantically involved with her. I pursued Alice with further questions.

'You never told me you were seeing him and I have the impression that there is more to this than you have revealed. Dare I ask if we are we all involved in a ménage-a-trois here?'

In avoiding the question Alice didn't give an answer but continued unloading her shopping.

'We are aren't we?' I pressed, 'So that is why you don't want a divorce from your husband,' I added.

'Okay, okay, your right, but I don't want to leave you Rick,' replied Alice.

'I thought that there were to be no more lies or secrets between us,' I said.

'Yes, that's true but how many times have you lied to me in the past?' asked Alice.

'Alice, that was a long time ago, but since we have lived together I haven't lied to you once,' I replied.

'I don't know that for sure,' remarked Alice.

'You may have to vacate here, because I can not sustain a situation whereby you are enjoying both your husband and me, yet living under my roof, so if you want to stay, then you will have to give him up,' I urged.

'I cannot do that,' insisted Alice.

'Then I'm afraid you will have to leave. Please collect your belongings and leave today,' I replied in anger.

Alice appeared upset by my decision and went upstairs to pack her bags. I began to think that history was repeating itself and that I was getting quite used to my partners leaving me to my solitude. However Alice had made the decision not to move quietly as I could hear a lot of unusual noises in the upstairs bedroom. When I investigated, I was met with the spectacle of Alice ripping up my shirts and suits to shreds in a revenge attack. In taking the initiative I moved across to stop her but she had already exerted maximum damage to my clothes. In a fit of anger and distress Alice ran out of the bedroom with her suitcase, down the stairs and out of the house. The last I saw of Alice on that day was of her erratically driving away on my drive weaving from side to side.

I was then left alone to contemplate the disastrous consequences of the discovery I had made and couldn't believe that I could have been so stupid. My naivety had precluded me from finding this out sooner. Although I was very hurt emotionally by what had recently happened I thought that Joy was also implicated and felt that I owed it to her to reveal what I knew.

A call to Joy was therefore necessary to alert her of my recent findings. Although Joy and I were barely on speaking terms, I felt I owed it to her to impart my recently discovered information. I knew that Joy had returned to her sister Sylvia so I made that my first port of call. I received the usual warm welcome from Sylvia and was invited in the house. As I was talking to Sylvia, Joy walked into the house. She was not quite so pleased to see me and got straight to the point by asking me what I was doing there.

'I understand you are seeing a person by the name of Herbert Long,' I said to Joy.

'So what if I am. I don't know how you found out Rick, but it's really none of your business,' insisted Joy immediately going on the offensive.

'Listen Joy, I'm not really interested in what men you wish to see. However I really must warn you that this man is married and still has regular contact with his wife,' I revealed.

'Rick, that's not news to me, he told me he was married,' confirmed Joy.

'Are, but did you know that he is still romantically involved with his wife and they see each other rather a lot. You could also be named as the reason for a break up in a divorce action,' I urged.

'Well you would say that, just to try and split us up. I don't know why you do this Rick. Anyway it's not going to work, so you can get back in your car and face it in the direction from whence you came,' insisted Joy with anger. When Joy was in that sort of mood there was no chance of convincing her about anything, so I did what I was asked to do and left. Sylvia meanwhile came out with me to the gate.

'I can't understand my twin sister, she seems to believe that anyone who offers advice has an ulterior motive,' said Sylvia.

'I know. Look Sylvia I have nothing to be gained by splitting her and Herbert Long up, but see if you can make her see some sense. She has already been badly let down by Wentworth who nearly stole almost all her money and it wouldn't do her or me any good if she was let down again,' I said.

'I will do what I can,' confirmed Sylvia, 'but she is rather headstrong and will only believe what she wants to believe.'

I left Sylvia to her thoughts and the task of trying to convince Joy that I had no ulterior motive for my visit.

Chapter 23 The Unwelcome Visitor

I had been working on the garden most of the day and the backbreaking job of weeding and lawn mowing was taking its toll on my body. I thought owed it to myself to treat my body to an early night.

It didn't take me long after hitting the pillow to fall into a deep sleep. Around one o'clock in the morning I was woken to a noise from the lower floor. In my half duped slumber I didn't take pay too much attention and turned over in the bed to see if I could return to my happy state of unconsciousness. I believed I had almost achieved this when I heard the distinctive sound of someone walking about downstairs.

'It must be an intruder. Not again,' I thought, *'Whatever happens, I must not repeat the same mistakes I made with Ralph Brown.'* I laid motionless in bed in the darkness frightened to move the smallest of muscles, hoping that my intruder would take what he wanted and leave. My interloper had other ideas, for I could hear him moving from room to room making no attempt to disguise the sound of his actions. I could hear cupboard doors being opened, the sliding of drawers and the odd thud where he or she had accidentally collided with a piece of furniture. Then I heard a volley of loud noises as if possessions were being smashed up. From the length of time taken, it appeared the intruder

had all the time in the world to forage and investigate the obvious and most likely valuables of his choosing.

Then my fears escalated as the intruder was heard climbing the stairs. I froze when I could hear doors opening as the person moved from bedroom to bedroom, again making no attempt to disguise any sounds of movement. I thought any moment this person will walk into my bedroom and I had no idea what the intruder looked like or whether he or she was in possession of a weapon. In order to deter an invasion of my privacy I switched on a bedside lamp, hoping that the light would prevent the intruder from entering the room.

I laid motionless in the bed, then without warning, I saw my bedroom door slowly opening and the beam of a torchlight streaming into the room. I waited with baited breath to see the identity of my intruder and was mortified when I saw a hooded person enter the room with a baseball bat swinging about in his hand. The hood on the person disguised the face and had eye slits cut out. The sudden vision of this spectacle was terrifying.

'Who are you, and what do you want,' I shouted nervously.

The intruder shone his or her torch into my eyes so that I received the full glare of the light forcing me to look away and shade my eyes with my hand. There was a long silence while I waited for an answer.

'You have a safe downstairs and I want the number of it,' the person yelled as he menacingly wielded the baseball bat as if to strike me with it, but not actually carrying out the threat. From the voice and shape of the intruder I knew that it was a male, but was unable to ascertain any distinctive features about him or his age.

'I'll give it to you but it's not going to be much use, because there's nothing in it,' I replied.

I started to give him the number together with the number of turns on the dial, whereupon he interrupted me obviously changing his mind by accepting my answer that the safe was empty.

'Where's the money then?' he asked, still terrorising me with the baseball bat.

'You will find about four hundred pounds in my green jacket hanging up in the wardrobe, please take it and go,' I answered hoping that would satisfy his requirements.

Without any further words he went to the wardrobe and started to pull clothes out at random dropping them uncaringly on the floor until he had found my green jacket. He then rummaged through all the pockets until he found my wallet and the money he was looking for.

'Okay have you got any more?' he asked.

'No, I haven't,' I answered.

'You'd better not be telling me any lies,' he said pushing the bat nearer to my face.

'I swear I'm telling you the truth,' I confirmed in fear.

'Well I'm going now, but I have to tell yer that you will need to get yourself a new telly and a new music centre,' he informed.

In listening to his voice during our exchange of questions and answers I thought I recognised the voice, but wasn't certain.

'Hang on, I do believe I know you,' I said.

The intruder who was about to leave the bedroom turned around to face me.

'No you don't,' he insisted.

'Yes, you are Zach,' I confirmed.

'That is not my name,' he said.

'No, but you have used it before as a pseudonym,' I argued.

The intruder ventured over to the bed holding the baseball bat high in the air as if to hit me with it.

'Listen if you value living on this earth a bit longer, you will not say anything about this to anyone. The slightest whisper and I'll be back,' he said.

The intruder then slammed the bat down on the pillow centimetres from my head causing me to jump sideways in fright.

He then slowly moved the bat across my cheek and started to push my nose up with it.

'You savvy?' he said still using the bat as a threat.

'Yes I understand,' I confirmed in my frightened state.

'Good, you can go back to sleep now,' he said removing the bat from my nose.

With that last comment my interloper left the bedroom kicking through the clothes that he had purposely dropped on the floor. I continued to listen as I heard him unplugging the electrical items he said he was going to take. The next thing I heard was the reception door opening and closing and he was gone.

I was dreading going downstairs to see what damage had been done while the intruder was searching for items of value. When I did eventually venture into the reception rooms, the damage was all too apparent. Chairs had been knocked over and some damaged in the course of being heavily handled or deliberately smashed. Drawers had been pulled out and lay broken on the floor. Ornaments were also damaged as they lay in pieces scattered in all directions. There was a drought coming from a lounge window, which on closer investigation had been removed from its hinges by the intruder to gain entry. I sensed that Jason had some involvement here, after all he had made a threat to me the last time I visited him.

A full morning was taken up clearing the damage caused by the intruder. The worst inconvenience my raider had inflicted on me was the lack of use of the missing items which he had stolen. I made a quick inventory of the destroyed or missing items and contacted my insurance company regarding the incident.

Chapter 24 The Drive

The following day after the robbery I took a drive into town to do some shopping. The journey took me down a series of country lanes, to which because of constant use, I had become very familiar of the topography of the area and the route going into town which included every twist, turn and tree along the way.

The day was pleasant, with the warmth from the sun penetrating through the window and adding to a general feeling of comfort and well being. As I continued my journey I looked in the rear view mirror and saw a large four by four land vehicle pulling out of a side road. Without taking too much notice of this vehicle which was now following me, I proceeded to take the first bend of a part of the road that I knew had a series of delicate twists and turns, which required a certain amount of driving care.

The vehicle behind me had by this time caught up to my family saloon and was quite close to my rear bumper. I waved him to pass me, but he seemed more interested in following me. I tried a different tactic accelerating to create more room between us, but found that the land vehicle was reciprocating every move I made. By the time I had reached the second bend, I felt a nudge on the bumper almost forcing me off the road. I had come to the realisation that what I was experiencing was not accidental, but a deliberate ploy to force me off the road or create a road disaster. Overcome with fear, my driving became faster and more erratic and I found I was losing a bit of concentration.

The next part of the road was straight which enabled me to apply sufficient acceleration to get clear of my pursuer. Then came another series of bends, which required me to brake and deliberate a slower speed in order to manoeuvre the turns in the road which I knew so well. With a brief look in the mirror I noticed that the chasing driver was close behind me and ready to ram the back of my car. I tried to accelerate, at the same time feeling an added surge forward, helped from a push from behind. Steadying myself from a quick reaction I was able to take the next bend although catching the side of my car on a tree, knocking off a side wing mirror and scraping the side of my car.

Looming up at me was another twist in the road which I tried to negotiate at speed, but was rammed again from behind thereby causing me to lose control of my vehicle. I tried to manoeuvre the car by turning the steering wheel away from the edge of the lane, but the push into my rear was sufficient to unstable my vehicle and I was forced off the road, somersaulting in the process. I ended up with the vehicle inverted in a ditch with the wheels still spinning as a result of the centrifugal force.

In the upside down position, with a released airbag in my face, I had difficulty in releasing my seat belt which was cutting into my chest. I looked around and noticed that my pursuer had stopped his vehicle, but had remained inside it. Moving closer to the window, I tried to spot the person who had put me in this dreadful predicament, but my vision was not clear so I could not identify or pick out any discerning features of the person in the land vehicle. However it wasn't long before I heard my attacker start his vehicle and drive off at a great speed leaving me to deal with my problem of escape.

After ten minutes of unsuccessfully trying to release myself from the seat belt, I heard a car stop and a man walked over to me and said the magic words.

'Are you alright mate? Can I be of assistance?' he asked.

'I'm trapped by my seat belt,' I said, 'can you try and release me?'

I felt the seat belt cutting into my chest due to the resistance of the weight of my body in the upside down position. The man wrestled with the clasp and managed to release the belt dropping me onto the ceiling of the car.

'You're bleeding rather badly on your head,' said my young helper.

I felt my head and found that blood was poring out of my temple, just above my right eye. Grabbing a handkerchief, I wrapped it around my head to try and stem the bleeding. With a bit of aid from my helper I managed to remove myself from the inside of the car. It was then that I saw the full horror of my disaster. The sides of the car were caved in, the roof was bowed under the impact and the hood of the car was flung open exposing an engine which was hissing with steam. I stepped further away from the car, which was just in time because it was encapsulated in a sudden ball of fire. The flames which were fanned by the wind, sent a black ball of smoke in the air with an acrid stench of burning rubber as the tyres started to burn.

'There's nothing more we can do here,' I said looking at the depressing site of my car going up in flames and smoke billowing high in the air and across the landscape. 'I think I'd better get checked out in a hospital.'

My young helper called for an ambulance on his mobile phone and I was rushed quickly to hospital. This was the third time that I had had an attack on my possessions which was having a devastating affect on me and all these occurrences were happening in close succession.

At the hospital I was checked over thoroughly by a junior Doctor who confirmed that I was not concussed in any way, but keen to ask me how I had sustained my injuries.

'Do you think you ought to get the police involved?' he asked.

'No, that's alright I really think it was an unfortunate accident,' I told him.

'Yes, maybe it was, but the driver never stopped, so it does become a crime and therefore you should inform the police,' he replied.

'No it's quite alright, I think I was probably more to blame than the other driver. In fact I may have even caused the accident. So you see I can't complain about the resultant damage to myself or my car,' I argued.

In giving my responses to the doctor I knew that it was pointless getting the police involved. I hadn't got the car registration number, didn't know the name of the driver of the land vehicle and even if I was aware of the identity of the road menace, it was his word against mine. There were after all no witnesses to what had happened.

Chapter 25 Meeting up with Zach

I realised since I last spoke to Jason I had become a target of his aggression and I wasn't prepared to take whatever he dished out to me and had to do something about it. I still had the telephone number of Zach so I thought I would give him a call.

'Hello, who is that?' said Zach.

'Is that Zach?' I asked.

'No there is nobody of that name here,' came the reply.

'This is Richard Wallace, you have done some work for me in the past when you called yourself Zach. Now I have some more work for you to do, so please call at my house and we will discuss what I have in mind,' I said.

'How do I know that you won't have the police waiting for me when I arrive,' he asked.

'Oh, if you are referring to the burglary that happened last month, I have no proof it was you, so you have nothing to worry about on that score.' I answered. 'So be at my house at three o'clock tomorrow. I can assure you that the pay for doing this job will be good,' I insisted.

'Okay, I will be there but you'd better not be wasting my time,' replied Zach.

The following day I waited for Zach. Three o'clock passed, then four o'clock and there was no sign of him. I began to give up all hope that he would arrive, then at approximately four thirty the door bell rang. I looked through the side window and saw Zach standing there.

'Come on in you're very late. I'd almost given up on you,' I commented.

'Well, you can't be too careful, I turned up late because I wanted to make sure that you hadn't double crossed me and that the old bill was not waiting to pounce,' reported Zach.

'Look Zach, I am being terrorised by Jason and I want to put a stop to it,' I said.

'I don't know about that, Jason is a friend of mine,' Zach replied.

'I understand what you say, but I thought there was no such thing as true friends in your business and I am prepared to sweeten the pill a bit with a generous inducement,' I said.

'Firstly, the robbery that had occurred at this house last month, which I knew was you, but did Jason have anything to do with it?' I asked.

'No he didn't, but you were right it was me. I'm telling you though, you will not be getting any of your stuff back and I aint gonna pay for any damage,' insisted Zach.

'Keep the goods you took, if you fulfil what I am about to ask you to do, you're welcome to them,' I replied.

'Now the person behind the road rage which also occurred last month, do you know if Jason was behind that incident?' I enquired.

Zach hesitated as if he didn't want to confirm my suspicions.

'He was behind it wasn't he,' I insisted.

'Yes, he was and he wanted me to tell you that he was responsible,' Zach blurted out.

'Do you know the maniac who was driving the vehicle?' I asked.

'No, I don't know but if I did I wouldn't tell. All I can inform you is that it wasn't me,' he confirmed.

'I thought Jason was behind it. He almost had me killed. Look Zach I'm looking to you to help me on this one,' I urged.

Zach looked at me in bewilderment and seemed to be lost for words.

'What do you want me to do?' he asked.

'Well I want you to teach him a lesson from me in the only way that Jason knows. It's no good me going to the police, because I know Jason and the softly softly approach doesn't appear to work with him. I'm sure you know some people in the same prison as Jason, who could help you persuade Jason that I am not a person to be messed with,' I suggested.

'Yes alright, I know what you are saying, I do know someone on the inside who may be able to help, but if he agrees, he will need paying also. I'll see what I can do,' replied Zach.

'Right I will give you one thousand five hundred pounds now and the same amount when you have done the job and report back to me. That should be sufficient to cover you and your accomplice,' I said.

'Okay, that seems a fair price, it's as good as done,' replied Zach.

I handed Zach the money which he carefully counted in front of me.

'Now, one more thing. If you ever attempt to enter this property again without my prior authorisation I shall be turning my reprisals on you and you know that I have the money to do it,' I warned Zach.

Zach seemed so pleased with receiving some money that he would have nodded in agreement to anything I asked of him.

One week went by and I received a visit from Zach.

'I've come to receive the rest of my dosh,' said Zach who believed in not displaying any airs or graces in his approach to requesting money.

'Not so fast, I have no proof that you have carried out what I asked you to do,' I insisted.

'Proof, if you want proof I have all the proof you want,' said Zach.

Zach threw down on the kitchen table some photographs which contained some rather gruesome images of Jason. On one, there was a picture of Jason with a broken nose and another showed him with two fingers missing off his right hand. I was mortified when I saw the terrible injuries inflicted on Jason that had in some way been instigated by Zach's instructions by another inmate in the prison. It was difficult to comprehend that I was the backer that had done this to a one time friend and lodger.

'You didn't have to go to these extremes,' I told him annoyed that he had gone to such a dreadful measure of violence.

'Look you wanted a job done, I have done it. He won't be bothering you again, so pay up as we had agreed,' insisted Zach.

I did as I was told, but felt uncomfortable that I had in some way was the catalyst that had inflicted these dreadful injuries and mutilation on another human being. It was then that I considered myself no better than Zach or Jason and was disgusted with myself that I had stooped to their level.

'Is Jason aware that you were behind his injuries?' I asked.

'No, he only knows that you are behind it, which is good because Jason and I can still remain friends,' replied Zach.

'You live in a very strange world Zach where there is no honour amongst friends and no respect in the law,' I said.

'Yep, that may be true, but it's only because of people like you that people like me are able to continue this style of life,' replied Zach.

Zach was right, I was instigating and perpetuating violence in my desperation to prevent further harm to myself. In his basic use of the English language he had succinctly explained the type of person I had now become. The stark reality of this nasty image of myself told me that I must never embark on such practices of retribution again.

*

Three months after meeting up with Zach, I was doing some shopping in the supermarket, when I was tapped on the shoulder. I looked around to see who was trying to attract my attention and was immediately shocked to see Jason. I quickly backed away expecting trouble from him and was surprised when he greeted me on friendly terms.

'Hello Rick, I hear that you have your own gang of vigilantes who are happy to cut and maim to your instructions,' he commented.

Not wishing to disappoint or prove Jason wrong I agreed with him.

'How did you know that?' I asked.

'Well, how do you think I got this?' replied Jason, holding up a hand with two missing fingers.

'Are you going to inform the police?' I asked.

'No. When, have I ever told the old bill anything,' he replied.

I tried to steer the conversation away from Jason's injuries and changed the conversation to something less controversial.

'When did you get out?' I asked Jason.

'Yesterday, when my appeal came up, I was able to satisfy the beak that I had a limited involvement with the robbery,' he replied.

'I suppose you will be looking to get your own back for your injuries?' I said.

'So that you can have another two fingers removed from me?' he queried. 'No as far as I am concerned, you'll get no more trouble from me.'

'So you think you may have learned a bit of sense,' I said.

Jason did not appear to want to further the discussion and carried on down the shopping aisle pushing his trolley. It was difficult to comprehend that the tit for tat, eye for an eye, method of achieving lawless satisfaction was now at an end and Jason had succumbed to the realisation that he had met a better match.

I finished my shopping and queued with my goods at the checkout. A voice behind me called out 'Hello Rick.' I looked behind and it was Sylvia.

'Fancy seeing you here,' she said looking in my trolley. 'Well you're not going to get fat on that,' remarked Sylvia. Why don't you come over to my place and I will cook you a proper meal.'

Sylvia had always been good to me, so not wishing to disappoint I readily agreed to her suggestion.

'Okay you're on,' I replied.

'Good,' she said, 'I'll see you at six o'clock this evening.'

Chapter 26 Family Visits

In the evening of the day that I saw Sylvia, I drove to her house as arranged. Sylvia greeted me warmly with a smile and sat me down in her lounge with a cup of tea while she continued cooking the dinner.

At dinner I seemed to be bombarded with a multitude of questions.

'I have been hearing about your escapades Rick, you seem to be having quite an eventful life,' observed Sylvia.

'You're right. Since I came out of prison I have been subjected to being accused of a murder I didn't commit, going on the run, sent to prison, violence from inmates, witness to a robbery in a bank, had my own house ransacked, involved in a car crash and had two women leave me,' I replied.

'I don't know Alice, but I do know my sister and her temper. I would say that Joy was not the right woman that you picked as a wife. I could tell that you have not been happy with her. Joy blows hot and cold and she doesn't deserve you,' related Sylvia.

It was noticeable that while Sylvia was talking she was being very tactile towards me, so I tried to change the subject.

'I see that you have never married,' I said.

'No, that is because I haven't found the right person,' replied Sylvia.

'Have you really tried?' I asked.

'Oh yes, I have had the odd fling but nothing too serious,' said Sylvia.

'Well you're an attractive woman, maybe you should try harder,' I suggested.

'I'm trying now,' she said as she put her hand on mine.

'If you mean what I think you mean, I am still married to your sister,' I confirmed.

'Yes, but that was a big mistake which I understand you are trying to rectify,' replied Sylvia.

I looked at Sylvia who being a twin, visually was a carbon copy of her sister and reminded me of the early days of my marriage with Joy which was probably the happiest time of my life.

'I tell you what. We will arrange to meet up for a day out and take it from there,' I told Sylvia.

I found Sylvia's approach embarrassing and believed that in making a tentative arrangement I had not committed myself.

Two days later I met up with Sylvia as arranged for dinner in a Thai restaurant. Although Sylvia was identical in appearance to Joy she was more gregarious and more cheerful than her twin. Sylvia often spoke about Joy and reported that while they were living in the same house they used to constantly argue. Joy was prone to telling lies and didn't do her fair share of the household chores, she confided.

I knew Joy better than anyone so I was aware that what I had heard was not open for dispute, but I wasn't sure why Sylvia denigrated her sister so much. It probably stemmed as far back as her childhood, but whenever it was, there was a definite loss of family ties.

'Tell me, how do you think the court case will go with Joy?' asked Sylvia.

'Well I hope it will clear my name,' I replied.

'Be prepared for Joy telling a few lies in court,' advised Sylvia.

'If she tells lies in court she will be found out and it could prove not to be to her advantage,' I argued.

'However thank you for your advice, I shall make sure the prosecution is made aware that there is a possibility that she may lie under oath,' I replied.

Our meeting up seemed to go well and in many ways we shared mutual compatibilities and we arranged to meet up for a single day in the following week. I was beginning to enjoy my days out with Sylvia, then one day as we were eating in our usual Thai restaurant, Joy and Herbert walked through the door. This, not surprisingly, caused an uncomfortable atmosphere between all of us.

Joy came over to our table and asked in her usual brazen way if they could sit with us.

'I'd rather you found a table of your own,' I replied.

'Rick is right, let's find another table,' said Herbert, at the same time attempting to drag Joy away by the arm.

'No,' protested Joy shrugging off Herbert's hand from her arm, 'I want to sit at this table.'

To everyone's astonishment she pulled out a chair and sat on it. Herbert, unable to restrain Joy followed suit. This was typical of Joy, conjuring up a situation in order to exacerbate embarrassment. I looked at Herbert who looked most uncomfortable about the predicament that Joy had placed him in. He didn't know where to look and started to play with the condiment receptacles on the table. We all looked at one another waiting for some one to speak.

'Well this is very cosy,' said Joy sarcastically.

'Now Joy, don't start, we have come out to enjoy ourselves,' I warned.

'I bet you have,' said Joy. Joy then turned her attention to Sylvia. 'How long have you been screwing my husband?'

Sylvia looked shocked at Joy's remark and immediately went on the offensive.

'Joy, you really are a vulgar person with a really disgusting mind. It's nothing like that, Rick and I have merely come out for a meal,' said Sylvia forcibly.

'Yes, I bet you have. Rick you will really have to be careful of my sister, she will have her claws in you before you know it,' informed Joy.

'Joy you left me almost three years ago, so it is really none of your business. Anyway I see that you have found someone else to spend your money,' I replied looking at Herbert.

Herbert appeared to be getting more and more embarrassed by the point scoring banter that was going on.

'Come on Joy, let's move to another table,' said Herbert.

'No, I am beginning to enjoy it here,' replied Joy, making herself comfortable by placing a serviette on her lap.

'Sylvia I suppose you will be milking my husband for every penny that he has got,' said Joy.

'Now Joy, that is quite enough. If you carry on like this, you will have to move to another table,' I insisted.

'I'm not moving anywhere,' confirmed Joy. 'Anyway my husband is useless in bed, but I expect you have found that out already,' said Joy.

'Right that is all I can take,' I replied. I left my chair and walked round to the other side of the table where Joy was sitting and started to drag her out of her seat in an effort to make her leave. Joy resisted by clouting me with a handbag about the face. I could see that I wasn't going to make Joy move so I returned to my seat. I had only just sat down when a pepper pot aimed by Joy caught me on my right temple.

A waiter seeing the commotion asked us all to leave. I was thankful that he had done this because Sylvia and I had endured enough of Joy's abuse which had no sign of abating. When we all reached the coolness of the fresh air, Joy continued with her insults until Herbert throughout his short time in the restaurant had remained silent, pulled Joy away in a separate direction. Herbert's reaction in halting the abuse created another argument between him and Joy. I watched as the two walked away giving each other a tongue lashing.

'Sylvia, do you see what I have had to endure?' I said.

'Yes, I feel sorry for Herbert,' replied Sylvia.

'That's a pity I was looking forward to the meal,' I said.

'Never mind, come back to my house and I will cook you something really special,' replied Sylvia.

Back at Sylvia's house I was treated to a very tasty Madras curry followed by apple pie. I sat on the settee bloated with all the goodies that Sylvia had put in front of me and thinking *'life doesn't get any better than this!'*

Sylvia finished clearing away the dishes and sat beside me.

'If Joy is going to accuse us of all these things, we had better not disappoint her,' she said drawing herself close to me.

Sylvia then put her arms around me and started kissing me passionately on the lips. I was glad she had done this because I could never have made the first move on her, being Joy's sister. I could see romance blossoming as a result of her bold actions, but I could also see a difficult situation developing. I gently moved Sylvia away from me.

'Look Sylvia, this could create huge problems between you and Joy, and I really don't want to do that,' I insisted.

'Rick, problems have existed between Joy and me for some time and I can never see that changing, so you don't want to have concerns over that,' replied Sylvia.

I had difficulty in making Sylvia understand that although I wanted to embrace the relationship, I could see Joy as a constant problem. She would have done all she could to split us up.

I left Sylvia's house with my mind in turmoil, for although I could foresee the problems that lay ahead I couldn't make Sylvia understand the difficulties that could be encountered in what I considered could be an incestuous relationship. Sylvia and I continued to meet up, because we enjoyed each others company, but there was no further romantic side to our liaisons.

Joy however was making life very difficult for Herbert in a way that I knew she would. When arguments existed between them, Joy would always phone Sylvia with a full detailed account of her problems and complaints.

*

It was a sunny Saturday and I wasn't working. I decided not to waste it and thought it might be a good idea to call on Sylvia and take a drive off somewhere.

When I arrived at Sylvia's house I knocked on the door, but no one answered, although I could hear a lot of raised voices coming from the house. I thought that it might be the sound on the television was too high which would account for her not hearing my arrival. I went around the back of the house and tried the rear door. It was not locked so I walked in. I was shocked to see Sylvia and Joy locking arms and legs on the kitchen room floor in an all out cat fight. There was hair pulling, scratching, punching, kicking and the banging of heads against the kitchen wall.

As these sisters were identical twins it was difficult to know which one was getting the worst treatment and which one had the upper hand of supremacy. Putting myself at danger I battled to separate the feuding sisters and in attempting to act as peacemaker, did not exactly come out unscathed. I had bruising on both my arms, a cut just above my right eye and a bleeding nose caused by a loose kick.

When I did manage to separate them, Joy armed herself with a few missiles in the form of cups, saucers and plates to which she set about aiming these at both Sylvia and me. This behaviour only stopped when Joy had run out of crockery.

'What is all this about?' I asked when household items had ceased flying through the air.

'It's Joy, she doesn't like the idea that you and I see one another,' said Sylvia.

'Yes, that's right. I know why you are doing it Sylvia. You are just doing it to get your own back on me,' said Joy.

'Listen Joy, there is no romantic entanglement between Sylvia and me, we just enjoy one another's company,' I said.

Joy looked around for something else to throw, but finding nothing immediately to hand went for the cutlery drawer. Then came a barrage of knives, forks and spoons which were coming in our direction so fast, it was difficult to dodge these dangerous metal objects. Although I was able to do a good job of ducking and side stepping, I managed to catch a fork which pierced my arm.

I was used to this sort of behaviour from Joy having been the victim of missile throwing when we were living together and the only way it would end was when Joy had physically expended her energy.

Blood started to pore from my arm so I wrapped some of Sylvia's towelling round it and also attended to the cut on my forehead. I looked at Sylvia and Joy and apart from a bit of bruising both of them had come out of their ordeal relatively unscathed.

'Look,' I said, 'I can't have you two women fighting over me.'

'You've got to be joking. Who in their right mind would want to fight over you?' replied Joy, who appeared so angry at the comment I had made, I thought she was going to start again.

I looked around at the kitchen which looked as though an elephant with a grudge had been let loose and done its worst in the place. Sylvia asked Joy to leave in tones that were not too polite. Joy did as she was told, but in her anger couldn't resist purposely knocking a few ornaments onto the floor to add to the rest of the breakages.

After Joy had gone, I stayed behind to help clear up the mess which took a good couple of hours to get the kitchen back to a near state of normality. Sylvia then made a pot of tea, but soon discovered that we had no receptacles to drink from. Joy had broken everyone in the house. This sudden realisation made us collapse on the sofa and laugh uncontrollably.

'Come on Sylvia, I came over here to take you for a drive and by golly that is just what I am going to do,' I said.

We drove off through the countryside, found ourselves a nice little teahouse where we stopped and had that long awaited cup of tea. I was halfway through eating a cream scone, when I heard a voice call out to me. I looked round and saw Janice from the Guest House sitting at another table with a female friend.

'Hello Rick, I thought I recognised the back of your head,' said Janice.

'Oh, it's lovely to see you again Janice. Is anything happening at the Guest House?' I enquired.

'Well, I do have your friend Jason staying there at the moment,' said Janice.

'I wondered where he was living. I hope he's not causing you any trouble,' I replied.

'No, he is as good as gold. He often talks about you Rick and seems to have a great deal of respect for you,' Janice confided.

I was pleased to hear these comments from Janice because I didn't want Jason to make a long term enemy out of me, particularly as we had been such good friends in the past.

After having my brief chat with Janice, I turned my attention to Sylvia.

'What are we going to do about that sister of yours?' I asked.

'Nothing,' replied Sylvia, 'we were never that close, and it wouldn't worry me if I never saw her again.'

'Sylvia, the court case will soon be upon us and Joy could be facing a prison sentence, doesn't that bother you as her sister?' I asked.

'Yes, I suppose it does. I wouldn't want her to go to prison,' replied Sylvia.

'Then I think you ought to attempt to make your peace with her,' I suggested.

'Perhaps you're right, but you know Joy, it won't be easy,' confessed Sylvia.

Our visit to the teahouse over, I said my farewells to Janice and her friend and took Sylvia back home and not wishing to overstay my time with her, I dropped her off at her gate and drove away.

I had planned to see my grandmother Edith. I hadn't seen her for some time and was mindful that I owed her a visit. Apart from Joy, she was after all the only living relative that I had in this country. Also after all the problems that I had recently encountered I needed to retreat somewhere away from the memories and the stress which constantly plagued my mind.

Edith was always pleased to see me and this visit was no exception.

'Hello Rick what have you been up to?' asked Edith.

'Oh, my life is really uneventful. Nothing has really happened since the last time I saw you,' I replied.

'But the last time I saw you was about five years ago and you can give no news of anything during that time?' queried Edith.

'No, I really do lead a boring existence,' I replied.

'It's strange I was reading a newspaper about three years ago, about a man who happened to have the same name as you, who killed a teenager and buried the body in a farmer's field. Isn't it a coincidence that he had the same name as you?' remarked Edith.

'Yes, very curious,' I replied.

'It gets better, I had the police calling on me at about that time, looking for a Richard Wallace,' said Edith.

'What did you tell them?' I asked.

'I told them that I did have a grandson by that name, but it wasn't the same person they were looking for. I also said that my grandson is a gentle person and would never kill anyone, so it couldn't have been him they were searching for.'

'Yes, you were right to tell them that,' I answered.

'Anyway you're not very good with the news Rick. How is that lovely wife of yours?' asked Edith.

'Oh she is okay,' I replied.

'Gosh Rick, it's like trying to get blood out of a stone,' said a frustrated Edith.

'Well I really haven't got much to report,' I replied.

'Much to report?' queried Edith, 'you've told me nothing.'

'Have you been in touch with your mother and father in Australia?' asked Edith.

'Yes, I have spoken to them. They are fine, although like you, I didn't have anything to report to them either,' I replied.

'Rick, you are impossible. I can't believe you have no news for me since the last time I saw you five years ago,' said an agitated Edith.

'Well, I do lead a bit of boring existence,' I replied.

I was beginning to wish I hadn't made my visit to Edith who had been desperate to receive some information from me. However, the kind of information I could have imparted, I was in no position to share. I believed that if Edith did know everything, it would probably cloud her opinion of me, which was something I didn't want to damage as her favourite grandson.

'Well as you lead such an uneventful and boring life, I have some news for you that might spice it up a bit,' said Edith.

I wondered what news Edith had that would have been of interest to me. After all she lived alone and as far as I was aware never saw anyone else during her monotonous existence.

'Approximately thirty eight years ago before you were born, your father had an affair with another woman,' related Edith.

'Did my mother know anything about this at the time?' I asked.

'No, she didn't and please don't interrupt,' said an agitated Edith.

'Then,' she continued, 'as a result of the affair a boy was born. I don't know what happened to the boy. He would be the same age as you, but it does mean that you have a half brother somewhere in this world.'

This was an astonishing story and I had to find out more.

'If you know the mother's name and I will try and find her,' I said.

'My memory is not as good as it used to be, but I think her name was Susan, yes Susan Long. However I can't remember the name of the baby that was born,' said Edith tapping her head as if trying to recall her memory.

'Come on Edith, you must remember,' I said frustratingly trying to get her to remember.

'No, it's completely gone from my mind, remember it was a long time ago,' said Edith.

'Was the name Herbert?' I asked.

'Yes, that's the name, Herbert,' she repeated, surprised that I had volunteered the correct name she was trying so desperately to remember, 'you knew all along didn't you Rick!'

'No, I surely did not, but I do know a Herbert Long,' I said, 'he lives somewhere near here and now I know who he really is, I shall do my best to track him down.'

'Did my mother know anything about the child being born? I queried.

'No she didn't although she did eventually find out about the affair between Susan Long and your father' said Edith.

'That's an amazing story, of the kind you only read in books,' I said.

When it came to saying my farewells to Edith I was reminded to come with more news on my next visit to her.

The visit proved to be a difficult experience and I found that while I was talking to Edith, her questions were a constant reminder of my dreadful past. Somehow, I had managed to keep my activities over the last three years away from Edith. In fact she didn't even know that I had been in prison. However the visit did in the end prove advantageous, as I did find out a bit of news about the family.

Two days after the rumpus at Sylvia's house I received a visit from Joy. When I answered the door she greeted me with a smile. As this manner of greeting was unusual for Joy, I invited her to come inside the house. Immediately I noticed from her body language that this was a different Joy to the one I had witnessed at Sylvia's house, but was curious to know why she had come to see me.

'Look Rick, I am due in court in seven days time and I would like you to do your best to drop the case against me,' begged Joy.

'Now, why would I want to do that, after having gone to so much trouble to have this court case arranged and spending a lot of money on it?' I asked.

'Because it could be damaging for me and I'm sure you don't want that,' she replied.

'You're right, I don't want that, but equally I wish to eradicate the stain on my character which can only be achieved if you admit to your part in Ralph Brown's death,' I pointed out.

'So I gather that you will not grant my request,' said Joy.

'No, and I will not do it. It has to take its course,' I insisted.

'Well Rick, you will be sorry you made this decision, because I will do my best to implicate you as the only person responsible for Brown's death,' threatened Joy.

'Joy you are forgetting one thing. I have already been tried for the murder of Brown, done time for it and subsequently released by the court of appeal, so whatever you say I can't be tried and punished for a second time over the same crime,' I argued.

'You will never get me to agree that I had any part in this,' said Joy.

I could now see Joy's mood changing back to her normal petulant behaviour. Having seen what she had accomplished at Sylvia's house in breaking all her crockery, I wasn't prepared to receive the same level of damage in my home.

'Listen Joy it doesn't appear that either of us are going to budge on this one. I also think we have said all that needs to be said, so let us leave it to the courts to come up with their own conclusions,' I insisted.

I was surprised when Joy, who was never stuck for an answer, offered no response and was even more surprised when she left my house quietly without incident.

The following day at work, I managed to retrieve from the Foreman the address of Herbert Long and that evening called round to his house. The main purpose of my visit was to relate to Herbert the information I had received from Edith.

Herbert was surprised to see me standing on his door step, but nevertheless invited me inside. Unfortunately when I walked into his lounge Joy was sitting in there.

'The reason I have come to see you Bert is that I have just received some information which directly affects you,' I said.

'What could you possibly tell me?' he asked.

'I have reason to believe that your mother and my father were at one time romantically involved and that you are the product of their illicit liaisons. Suffice to say you are my half brother,' I related.

'Don't listen to him Bert, he is trying to split us up,' yelled Joy. Joy stood up and started to walk over to me waving her arms in her anger.

'No, Joy. Sit down and let him finish,' said Herbert who was aware that I had now obtained his curiosity.

'I know it sounds like a farcical story, but if I were to tell you the name of your mother, would you believe me,' I urged.

'Yes, go on,' replied Herbert.

'The name of your mother is Susan Long who brought you up on your own. Now you can check this with your mother if you wish,' I said.

Herbert looked stunned and didn't know what to say. Joy in the meantime was getting really agitated about what I had told Herbert and couldn't contain herself any longer.

'I told you Bert, I know his game he is trying to cause problems between us,' bellowed Joy.

'No wait, I believe he is telling the truth. How else would he have known my mother's name,' said Bert.

'You realise now that Joy is your sister-in-law,' I pointed out.

'Yes, you may be right but you do also realise that Alice is also your sister-in-law,' he replied.

'True, but I have to tell you that I no longer see Alice. Unlike you, who is seeing Alice and Joy,' I said.

Joy immediately picked up on what I had said and immediately rounded on Bert.

'Is this true Bert?' yelled Joy.

Bert looked at me then looked at Joy.

'Yes he is right,' confirmed Bert.

Joy picked up her handbag, went over to Bert, slapped him around the face and stormed out of the house leaving the two of us astonished, looking at one another.

'How did you find out about this information,' asked Bert.

'Your grandmother or our father's mother told me,' I replied.

'What do we do now?' asked Herbert.

'Well there was a time when we enjoyed each others company, and I do believe that we can forget our differences, but this time see and appreciate each other as brothers,' I suggested.

'Yes I would like to return to how things were between us,' agreed Bert.

I left Bert's house satisfied that I had achieved some satisfactory conclusions. I had managed to convince Joy that her partner had been cheating on her and at the same time gained a brother.

*

As I no longer had a close relationship with Alice after the discovery that she had been seeing her husband without my knowledge, I was aware that she would not have the same interest in the impending court case. However, it was doubtful that she would have continued to use me as a client and therefore essential that I directed my attentions to finding an alternative solicitor.

A letter written to Alice explained the position to which she must have been previously fully aware. I approached a Solicitor by the name of Thomas Dingle and requested Alice to submit all the documentation on the case to him. Alice obligingly followed my instructions but sent me an enormous bill against her limited efforts towards preparation of the case.

The only request I made to Thomas Dingle was that we were to use Cleaver to act for the prosecution.

Chapter 27 Joy in Court

The day of the court case had finally arrived and in consideration of the varied and extreme vagaries of my life I regarded the day with prime importance. Joy had engaged a top class lawyer in the name of Hogan Bentley. The Crown prosecution was being covered by Cleaver, the same lawyer who defended me in the last case. Proceedings started to move quite quickly and Joy was called to the dock to give her evidence.

I looked around the court to see if there was anyone I knew. I immediately recognised three people, Dianne Brown, Ralph's mother and Herbert Long, my old working companion and brother. Both of them offered mixed expressions, Dianne would look at me as if she wished me dead and Herbert expressed a grin and a gesture of thumbs up to me. I wasn't sure who he was supporting today, but assumed it wasn't Joy.

In a second glance around the court house I managed to pick out Alice and I thought it was strange that she was not sitting next to her husband Herbert Long. As they were seated so far apart I could only assume that the ménage a trois that once existed between the three of us was well and truly over.

The judge commenced.

'Please state your name in full.'

'Joy Lillian Wallace,' Joy said nervously.

'Joy Lillian Wallace, you are charged with the murder of Ralph Brown on 3rd June 2000. How do you plead?' asked the judge.

'Not guilty,' said Joy.

Joy was then asked to take the oath.

Bentley rose to his feet and requested that Joy described, in her own words, her version of what happened on that fateful night of 3rd June.

'My husband had just been released from prison and after an exhausting drive home we were tired and went to bed early. My husband Rick woke up in the night and thinking that he heard some noises downstairs left the bed and went to investigate,' related Joy.

'What were you doing at this time?' asked Bentley.

'Oh, I was asleep when he went downstairs,' answered Joy.

'Please continue,' requested Bentley.

'A loud commotion in the garden woke me up. I looked out of the window and saw Rick, my husband with a knife in his hand having an argument with Ralph Brown. Then with one swift action Rick lunged into the body of Brown with the knife stabbing him in the chest,' said Joy.

'What happened then,' requested Bentley.

'Brown fell to the ground on his front and Rick plunged the knife into his back ensuring that he was dead. Rick then dragged the body into the house,' said Joy.

'Where were you when all this happened?' asked Bentley.

'I was still in the bedroom looking out of the window,' replied Joy.

'Did you at any time own a crimson carpet with a blue diamond inlayed into the fabric?' asked Bentley.

'Yes, we did own such a carpet,' replied Joy.

'It is this item of internal furnishings which categorically links you or your husband to this crime,' said Bentley. 'How did this happen to be found in the temporary grave of Ralph Brown?'

'Rick dragged the body inside the house, like I said and wrapped it in the carpet and then moved both carpet and contents into the garage,' continued Joy.

'When did you leave the comfort of your bedroom and come downstairs,' asked Bentley.

'I came into the lounge just in time to see Rick wrap the body in the carpet,' replied Joy.

'What happened next?' requested Bentley.

'Rick transferred the body to the garage,' replied Joy.

'Did he do this on his own,' asked Bentley.

'Yes, he did,' answered Joy.

'What happened after the body was placed in the garage,' asked Bentley.

'We both went back to bed and the following day Rick put the body in his car and drove off,' said Joy.

'Did you assist him in any way?' asked Bentley.

'He did ask me for my help but I wouldn't give it, telling him that he should phone the police,' said Joy.

'Why didn't you phone the police?' asked Bentley.

'My husband wouldn't let me,' replied Joy.

'That is all. No further questions,' said Bentley and sat down.

Cleaver for the Crown rose to his feet and addressed the Judge.

'Your Honour, some new evidence has come to light. May we take a short recess?'

'Yes,' we will reconvene at two o'clock,' ordered the Judge.

Outside the court Cleaver grabbed my arm.

'What's going on? The story unveiled by your wife is totally different to the statement you made two years ago,' queried Cleaver.

'Yes, I know. She is lying under oath,' I informed Cleaver.

'Is everything that she said a complete pack of lies?' asked Cleaver.

'Pretty much so,' I confirmed.

'So in some parts she was telling the truth. Tell me the parts where she was not lying,' said Cleaver as he stood there with a pen and pad in his hand.'

'She was right about me rolling the body in the carpet. She was right that I put the body in the garage. She was correct that we went to bed after I had done this and she was right that I had driven off with the body the next day. Everything else, as you will undoubtedly compare with the original statement I made, was a complete fabrication. Ralph Browns death certainly did not occur in the garden,' I confirmed.

'Tell me, if you looked out of your bedroom window, could you get a clear view of the garden?' asked Cleaver.

'No you couldn't. There was a tree in the way. I meant to have it chopped down because it obscures the light in the bedroom, but hadn't got round to doing it yet,' I told Cleaver.

'Right,' said Cleaver confidently, 'I think we are ready for Court.'

At two o'clock we all returned to court.

Cleaver summoned his first witness which was Dr. Phelps who originally examined the body.

'Doctor did you examine the body when it was retrieved from the temporary grave?' asked Cleaver.

'Yes I did,' confirmed Phelps.

'Did you also examine the carpet,' asked Cleaver.

'Yes I did,' confirmed Phelps.

'Can you tell us what you saw on the carpet,' asked Cleaver.

'Apart from it having a distinctive diamond pattern on a red background very little,' commented Phelps.

'Was there any blood on the carpet? asked Cleaver.

'Oh, yes the carpet took a lot of blood,' said Phelps.

'Doctor Phelps you reported the last time this came to court that one of the knife wounds would have pieced the aorta artery, which undoubtedly would have caused a lot of blood. Having regard for this where would you have said that the crime took place? That is on the carpet in the house or outside in the garden?' pressed Cleaver.

'The aorta artery is the main artery that comes from the heart. When someone dies the heart stops pumping, thereby reducing the blood flow around the body or in this case out of the body. There was too much blood on the carpet to suggest that the crime could only have been carried out on this floor covering,' confirmed Phelps.

'Thank you Doctor Phelps, no further questions,' said Cleaver.

Bentley then rose to his feet.

'Doctor Phelps. Your credentials are well known so we won't go into them. However the carpet you examined was crimson and would have contained dried blood. How therefore can you be sure about the saturation content of the carpet?' asked Bentley.

'Dried blood is not crimson like the carpet, it is a completely different colour, almost like a dark brown. Saturation was that bad that it had come through to the back of the carpet covering at least seventy five percent of the floor covering,' confirmed Phelps.

'Thank you, no further questions. You may step down,' said Bentley and sat down.

'I would like Mrs. Joy Wallace to take the stand,' said Cleaver.

Joy moved slowly and nervously into the witness box.

'Mrs Wallace it would appear from what you have told us under oath that you were nowhere near the victim when he was stabbed. In fact you seem to distance yourself from the entire incident,' said Cleaver.

'That is correct,' said Joy, 'I saw the whole incident in the garden through the window in my bedroom.'

'Even though it was pitch black outside you noticed that your husband had a knife? asked Cleaver.

'Well it wasn't too clear,' said Joy, 'but I did see something glistening in his hand.'

'I will agree with you Mrs Wallace that it wasn't too clear at all, because there is a large horse chestnut tree obscuring your window. So I put it to you that the darkness combined with the tree blocking your window, you wouldn't have been able to see anything in the garden,' Cleaver pointed out.

'Now,' continued Cleaver, 'Doctor Phelps has already established that the crime was committed in close proximity to the carpet. Do you wish to change your story?'

'Well it did happen a long time ago. It is difficult to remember. I may have got some things wrong,' said Joy.

'However you did say that you witnessed the incident and I do believe you, but what you saw was in the lounge,' said Cleaver.

'Well yes, you may have been right there,' said Joy now realising that the evidence was against her.

'So let's start again shall we, now knowing that I have jogged your memory,' insisted Cleaver.

Joy then started to revise her story.

'I heard a noise which I thought was in the kitchen and woke Rick up. He went down the stairs and I followed him. Rick went into the kitchen and I walked into the lounge. I heard a noise behind me turned round and was confronted with Ralph Brown. I screamed. Brown put his hands around my neck and began squeezing until I was unable to breathe. Rick heard the commotion and rushed behind him with a knife and Brown fell to the floor,' Joy related.

'When did you pick up the knife,' Cleaver asked.

'Oh, I never had the knife, Rick had a knife,' argued Joy.

'I'm not talking about the knife that Rick held which according to forensics did not create any life threatening damage. I am referring to the knife that you held.

'I didn't have a knife,' said Joy.

'Then how do you explain a knife wound to the upper chest, after all Brown was facing you and not Rick,' argued Cleaver.

'Rick may have knifed him again while he was on the floor,' explained Joy.

'Unlikely, because if he dropped like a stone, then it must have been as a result as a more serious wound to the front of the body carried out at the same time as the less serious wound to the back of the body which, we are informed made no serious or deep penetration,' pointed out Cleaver.

'Now let's move onto the transportation of the body from the lounge to the garage. You have already confirmed that you had no part in moving the body,' said Cleaver.

'That's right I did say that,' agreed Joy.

'Now, Brown was a big man and weighed approximately two hundred and ten pounds. The carpet was of a dense quality and weighed approximately one hundred pounds. Can you explain to me how a man who weighs one hundred and ninety pounds can move a combined weight of a body and a carpet weighing three hundred and ten pounds from the lounge to the garage, a distance of twenty yards completely on his own without any assistance at all,' Cleaver pointed out.

'I wouldn't like to say,' said Joy.

'I dare say you wouldn't. We will let the Jury decide on the probabilities on that one,' said Cleaver.

'I have no further questions,' said Cleaver sitting down.

The court then had a recess and everyone returned the next day for the summing up.

The Judge advised that they mustn't let their hearts rule their heads in this case but must come to their conclusions based on the evidence they had heard.

Bentley rose to give his summing up.

'This is an unusual case because this has already been to trial once and Richard Wallace was accused of Ralph Brown's murder and sentenced to life imprisonment. However he is not on trial here today, but it does beg the question that if someone was found responsible for a crime two years ago, what has changed to make it any different now. It is true that the only evidence linking the person involved in the crime is a crimson carpet with a distinctive fluorescent pattern inlaid in the fabric. Although there was some confusion in Joy Wallace's story.   In a revision of what she has told us, it does appear to tally with the statement her husband made two years ago when this first came to trial and Richard Wallace was condemned to prison as a direct result of the statement and admissions that he had made in the trial.   I therefore truly believe that there is only one conclusion you should come to and that is to find the defendant Mrs Joy Lillian Wallace not guilty of the murder charge against her.'

Bentley sat down and Cleaver left his seat for his summing up.

'At no time should we link Richard Wallace's name to this case. My learned friend has recently pointed out, Richard Wallace is not on trial here.   However it is difficult not to mention his name because he had been complicit in removing the body and trying to dispose of the evidence, but he was not responsible for killing Ralph Brown.   During the trial we have been able to expose the tissue of lies under oath that Joy Wallace made throughout the trial. The rumpus in the garden, the stabbing, her part in moving of the body from the lounge to the garage.   All of these topics received a different elucidation when the evidence was stacked against her.   I put it to you members of the Jury that there is only one outcome to this trial and that is a guilty verdict.'

Cleaver took his seat.

The Judge then addressed the Jury.

Members of the Jury, you have all heard the evidence and the changed testimony by Mrs Wallace to a plea of self defence against a violent attacker. If you feel that the stabbing exerted by Mrs Wallace was a justified act of self preservation and not premeditated in any way, then it would be advisable and quintessential to return a not guilty verdict.

The Jury retired from the court.

I saw Cleaver afterwards who seemed quietly confident of his performance.

'How do you think it went Mr. Cleaver,' I asked.

'I'm not sure. It is all up to the Jury now. Alice will let you know when the Jury has come to a conclusion and when we are due back in court,' confirmed Cleaver.

Two days later I was informed by Alice that we were due to return to Court at ten o'clock.

The long awaited time had come.

The Judge asked the foreman to stand and give his verdict. The foreman rose to his feet.

'We find the defendant Mrs. Joy Lillian Wallace not guilty of murder.'

I looked at Cleaver and then Alice as if I hadn't rightly heard what he had said.   There were a few murmurs in the court.

Then the foreman continued.

We believe that the defendant acted in self defence. However we make this proviso that the defendant is guilty of falsifying evidence under oath.

Thank you members of the jury,' said the judge, 'this court will reconvene tomorrow for sentencing.'

The following day the judge sentenced Joy for two years imprisonment for falsifying her testament under oath.

In a way I was pleased that Joy never received a long sentence and managed to get off the murder charge, she was after all trying to protect herself.

For my part I achieved what I had set out to do, having been completely vindicated of a murder I did not commit, saved by the evidence contained on a bespoke blue fluorescent diamond, inlaid on a crimson carpet.

-------------------------- The End--------------------------------